Still

a memoir

Julia Kelly

NEW ISLAND

STILL
First published in 2025 by
New Island Books
Glenshesk House
10 Richview Office Park
Clonskeagh
Dublin D14 V8C4
Republic of Ireland

newisland.ie

Print ISBN: 978-1-83594-008-2
eBook ISBN: 978-1-83594-009-9

British Library Cataloguing in Publication Data. A CIP catalogue record for this book is available from the British Library.

Product safety queries can be addressed to New Island Books at the above postal address or at info@newisland.ie.

Set in 11.75 on 15 pt in Adobe Caslon Pro
Typeset by Compuscript Limited, compuscript.com
Cover design by Luke Bird
Printed by Finidr, Czech Republic, finidr.com

New Island received financial assistance from The Arts Council (An Chomhairle Ealaíon), Dublin, Ireland.

New Island Books is a member of Publishing Ireland.

10 9 8 7 6 5 4 3 2 1

For Nick, David, Alexia and Beany

I want to be a wave breaking
On the shores of undiscovered land

—NICK KELLY, 'HORSE WATER WIND'

Before

YOU'RE NOT IN THE KITCHEN, WHERE I WANT YOU TO BE. The air smells of your perfume and of burnt toast. On the table there's a charred crust at the edge of a plate full of scrapings; one of your white hairs is coiled on a knife smeared with marmalade and butter and beside the plate there's a cheque made out to Member in Charge. It's payment of a speeding fine; even the letters of your name seem in a rush, the D of Delphine so slanted it's almost prone.

Punctuality isn't as important to you as your unspoken determination to arrive anywhere before anyone else, thereby appearing not just dependable but very much on top of things. As well as the cheque, there are two envelopes beside the burnt toast – one for the gardener, the other for the cleaner – addressed in the same rushed hand. Beneath these, in a transparent plastic folder, is the itinerary for your next trip.

It's the fifth of February 2012, two days before you depart for Ecuador to visit the Galápagos Islands. I can't remember where you said you would be this morning – aqua-aerobics, someone's funeral, Ballyogan dump? – because I hadn't been listening. I used to plead with you to listen to me. I took comfort in your encompassing hugs and your endless reassurance that it would be OK, pet, but I never felt that I had your full attention; your pale eyes were always focused on something beyond me.

'No, you listen to me,' my daughter says these days, dominant though diminutive, small hands on small hips. It's true that my brain takes breaks when people are talking, especially when it's you about your trips. They are dizzying in their detail and in their frequency. 'Did I not tell you about the morning we sailed down the Ganges?' you will begin, and I don't want to suppress your enthusiasm by saying that you have in fact told me, at least twice, so I let you continue, intermittently nodding and frowning while thinking of other things. Even if I say yes, that you have told me all about whatever trip it was, you will carry on regardless, with brio and a sort of ruthlessness that is becoming more evident as you age.

I fill the kettle the lazy way, through the spout and to the brim. I don't want tea but I like the reassuring sound of the hot water bubbling and the warmth of its diminishing steam. Above the kettle and hidden behind the old Chinese box containing teabags is an almost empty packet of custard creams. You've twisted the wrapper tight, not so much to keep the biscuits fresh but as a way of making them trickier to access. You'll succumb to them this evening, when you're alone and sleepy; you'll jiggle them lightly in your cupped hands while watching the news, occasionally lifting your legs off the footstool and scissoring them vigorously, for a few seconds in mid-air in a desultory attempt at exercise.

I flop down on the bench side of the table, then lie back on its sun-faded foam cushions, causing the dull odour of countless backsides to escape and dust to dance in a funnel of low winter light. Their toffee-coloured covers are identical to the ones we had in our old family home; the table itself seems the same, though its orientation is different. I'd viewed the underside of that table more than the top when I was growing up: I liked to slump beneath it when I was monumentally bored or sulking about some great injustice. In a sloth-like teenage state one day I noticed, while picking at an ancient piece of gum someone had deposited there, that our kitchen table wasn't actually a table at all but a door: builders' illegible measurements had been scrawled in red along the edge and there was a circular hollow halfway down where the handle should have been.

The phone rings, which makes me move – not towards it to answer it, but in the opposite direction and out of the room. No one knows I am here, not even you, so I feel under no obligation to pick it up. I'd let myself in; I don't remember when or why you entrusted me with a key – perhaps it was before your last trip, so that I could punch in the code of the temperamental house alarm if it went off while you were gone, which it always did.

Twice lately you didn't hear me when I rang the doorbell, immediately presenting my brain with a very plausible disaster, the one I've been dreading and predicting since Dad died: that you had collapsed in the garden when trying to start the lawnmower, or choked on a cream cracker while doing your Italian homework, or fell asleep in the bath and slid silently underwater. I continued to catastrophise until you appeared, visibly irritated by my anxiety when you had just gone to spend a penny, for crying out loud.

*

Dad's death when you were just fifty was a sad liberation for you. It gave you a chance to live the life you had wanted, to come out of your shadowy existence in the kitchen, where you worked in a permanent haze of smoke that seeped from the grease-layered oven you neither had the time nor the desire to clean. Now that you no longer had to cook for your husband, and your children were mostly grown, you could start making some of your own plans and accomplishing things for yourself. Along with the ever-increasing number of stamps on your passport and your diplomas, certificates and degrees, you have accumulated so many friends since becoming a widow that it's a full-time occupation just to make time for them. You aren't especially rigorous in your selection criteria and have encouraged the company of some fairly eccentric and tricky human beings. You not only suffer fools, you invite them in and make them a cheese soufflé. Now, as you all age, some of these friends are becoming ill and dying; death has started to follow you around like a miserable inconvenience, getting in the way of your travel plans, stealing people you like in sudden slamming crashes and collapses or in long-drawn-out hospital stays, where you are forced by your sense of loyalty to visit them and watch them becoming bird-like and bald, sunken on pillows and then gone.

'I'm no good at death,' you said to me last summer, not wanting to break a commitment to visit a friend in Germany when in Dublin one of your oldest friends was terminally ill and given just days to live. After a lot of badgering from me and my siblings, you cancelled the trip and remained at home till her inevitable death and funeral.

On the next holiday you had scheduled that same summer – to Italy with your children and grandchildren – you were uncharacteristically grumpy and sullen. You adopted a solitary and rigid routine, drinking your milky tea alone on the swing seat in the mornings, having a swim in the pool before the little ones dive-bombed in, and driving to the nearby town to look around the market unaccompanied.

Even this solitude didn't give you peace of mind. Everything that holiday seemed to anger you: the escalators up to the Etruscan hill town broke down or were turned off without warning or any logic that you could see and you'd had to struggle up the high, immobilised metal steps in forty-degree heat, pausing regularly to catch your breath, creating a queue of impatient, spritely Germans and Americans behind you.

And when you tried to run me over on that holiday I finally knew your anger wasn't directed at me. I'd asked you to collect some page proofs of a book I was working on when you had finished looking around the market; I'd sent them to the local print shop. You had returned without them and when you saw the disgruntled expression on my face, you looked for a moment like you might slap me. Instead you got straight back into the car and drove towards me at speed. I jumped out of the way, horrified and you kept on driving, along the rickety flagstones of the complex, through the electric gates and away.

You cried when you kissed me on the head that evening, having returned from wherever you had been. You said that your own mother had died at seventy-three, and you were almost seventy-one. It was an odd form of explanation, but I understood. You were annoyed and frightened by the proximity of death when there was still such a lot to do.

*

The trip to the Galápagos is less because of the giant tortoises and more because you have run out of other places to visit. Since the surprise holiday to India my siblings and I gave you for your sixtieth birthday and the subsequent sale of our old home giving you a sizeable income for the first time in your life, your feet have barely touched the ground. You've been to China, South Africa, America many times, and back and forth to Europe almost monthly.

You never admit to a fear of flying though you swiftly bless yourself, like you do when passing any church, as the plane rattles and sways and picks up speed and the undercarriage pulls up. Here we go, here we go, here we go, I sing to myself just as habitually at take-off, trying to trick my brain into believing that I'm excited rather than petrified and convinced that I am on a doomed flight, statistics doing nothing to console, nor your reminding me that I would be more likely to die from being kicked in the backside by a donkey. I blame you for this phobia – you and Dad, in fact – two otherwise intelligent and entirely rational human beings who always flew separately as soon as you became parents, so that we would not be left orphaned in the event of a sudden loss of cabin pressure and a hurtling plummet to earth.

*

The rusty old clothes horse is balancing in an A-shape across the top of the bath. Your black Speedo swimsuit is draped over it and dripping. You have baths like others take showers – in and out in five minutes, never lingering, despite the deep water and the capful of Radox that you always add; foam still clings to your damp red ankles while you hurry to get dressed. Your white bathing cap, whose rubbery texture I would have very much enjoyed chewing as a child, hangs off the edge of the clothes horse. It's embossed with white roses, just like your wedding dress was, and the frosting on your wedding cake. 'You must deadhead those roses,' you say in the summer, violently snapping off the wilting petals with your garden-gloved hands, 'to encourage more blooms.' You brush the hair from your face with the back of a mud-encrusted, oversized glove, while silently surveying the garden for the next thing to attack.

Now I remember. You said you were going swimming this morning, with your best friend, on Greystones beach – so you'd been back and dashed out again, as you do. Tall, thin, Church-of-Ireland and slow-moving, this woman is the opposite of you in many ways but is the only person you don't have to adjust your voice for when talking on the phone. You speak instead in a flat monotone, as you would to one of your children, because you are so comfortable in her company.

Your favourite thing is to swim in the sea. You've been swimming in it since you first learned, in the inky still water around Garnish Island in Glengarriff, where you would go with your parents as a child. You swim at Greystones as often as you can, undressing at the beach with the insouciance of old age, flat posterior in the air, never bending at the knee, a habit which irritated me enormously and unfairly.

Wearing latex swimming socks to protect your vulnerable toe, the one that's missing its nail, you pick your way over loose stones towards the sea, looking ahead at the horizon. Chin up, fingertips daintily skimming your thighs, you intermittently flex your hands and turn them out like the ballerina you once wanted to be. You are still graceful despite your full figure, still youthful despite your age. You wade into the water, tentative but silent. Slowly you submerge yourself – feet, knees, thighs – then you're in, with a contented exhale (you will never admit to the breath-grabbing shock of the cold) and you begin a languorous but effective breaststroke, moving parallel to the shore, neck strained upward, slow and steady, circular rings of glassy water pulsating outwards as you progress. You stay in for as long as you can tolerate the frigid water. Even when your friend is back on the beach, goose-pimpled, with dripping hair and rigorously towelling herself, you still tread water or flip onto your back – isn't this heavenly, you say, though no one can hear you – and search the cloud-filled sky for the patch of blue you always find there.

*

There's a draught coming from the bedroom; it's causing the open door to judder at irregular intervals against its timber frame. I go in, close and bolt the window, grab the cardigan – cashmere, duck-egg blue – that's hung over the dressing-table chair and put it on. We exist at different temperatures – you forever wanting fresh air, me eternally too cold.

On the bedside table beside an empty mug with a clump of dried milk on its rim is a photograph of my father, in a corroded silver frame. I had a copy of the same photo that I hid down the side of my mattress when he was dying. On the reverse I'd written the things I had never said to him – that I loved him, that I was sorry for being such a pain in the backside and for putting ten years on his life – though I'd whispered all of this in his ear too, when he was curled stiff with rigor mortis. Hearing was the last sense to go, the nurse said.

The open suitcase on the bed is already partly packed. It's the smallest of your three Samsonite cases, a gift from some of the women you often travel with. The medium and large ones have yet to be used – even though a three-week trip demands more space, you will manage with the smallest; to travel with anything larger you deem wildly impractical and extravagant. You are quietly competitive about this too – needing to be the most sensible traveller in your group.

You have assembled all the clothes you will be taking and have rolled rather than folded them (to prevent creasing and to allow for more space) in colour-coordinated rows. They are mostly made from the silk you bought on your visit to India – it's wonderfully practical, you always say. You never bothered to use the Colour Me Beautiful consultation you were given for one of your birthdays; you know instinctively the shades that suit you – creams, pale blues, taupes, dusty pinks – and wear trousers that categorically don't: Lady Diana-style beige chinos, too flesh-like to be flattering, cropped and tapered at the ankle, making you look larger around your middle. You've bought T-shirts in five different colours for the trip, from that expensive shop in Blackrock, and will pack one formal outfit just in case – you have hung the various options on hangers outside your wardrobe. When you get home you'll ask me which one I think would work best (though I know you have already decided), holding the dress against yourself and adopting your mirror pose: chin up, chest out, one leg pointed in front.

All your toiletries are practical too, travel-sized and already in a see-through and sealed plastic bag, ready for inspection at airport security. In a smaller pile, on top of an unintentionally trendy North Face rucksack that must be for hand luggage, are a plastic money belt, a silk scarf for the respectful visiting of chapels and for tying at a jaunty angle around your neck to finish off an outfit (as you always recommend to me – advice that I've never once heeded), a new Maeve Binchy novel and those wretched stockings you hate wearing, the ones that prevent deep-vein thrombosis.

In a row along the wall you have lined up several pairs of impossibly small walking shoes and a new pair of runners, navy with white laces. For reasons I don't understand, the sight of these runners makes me suddenly dread ever having to lose you. Beside these is the ancient tan-coloured case you keep your medicines in. It's filled with out-of-date and potentially toxic tablets and tonics, its cardboard lid has collapsed and is covered in dust. It was kept out of reach at the top of a mahogany chest in your bedroom for all of our childhoods. I used to balance on a chair and yank it down to help myself to a few chewy orange-flavoured Rubex vitamins when there were no good snacks left in the kitchen.

Unlike most of your once-sporty friends, you have no arthritis and have never been in hospital (all of your five children were born in a nursing home) aside from when your ingrown toenail was removed. You have been trying to get fit ahead of the Galápagos trip. Your best friend doesn't want you to go; she thinks it's too challenging a journey for someone who is overweight and has high blood pressure. But you tell her and anyone else who seems concerned that aside from your sea swimming, you have been doing aqua-aerobics twice a week and walking around Blackrock Park for thirty minutes at a time, trying to catch up with walkers ahead of you and sometimes overtaking them.

*

I look at my watch and chew at the side of my thumb the way my father used to do when he was worried.

When I try to call you to see where you are, your phone goes immediately to voicemail, which suggests that you are talking to someone rather than that it's turned off.

Downstairs again, I go into the drawing room, with its airy, under-used feel, and stand at the window wondering whether to wait for you or set off for home. Though it's a different house on a different street and at a different time, as I stand at the window and look out at the stark trees in the porridge-grey light, hoping to spot you, I'm reminded of the torturous hours we had watched and waited as children for you and Dad to return from wherever you'd gone without us. You travelled without us often and our excitement at your expected return was never about gifts, of which there were often none, or else they were traditional dolls with oddly sparse hair or miniature German dictionaries. It wasn't even the reprieve your return gave us from the irritating habits of homesick au pairs. What we wanted back was you and Dad in your selves with your coughs and walks, your smells and sounds, and your very particular way of being.

'You'd swear I was going to the moon,' you always said when we whined about you leaving. And there we would wait, kneeling at the low dining-room window, focused at first and full of anticipation, hearing the silvery rush of wheels along wet roads of each approaching car, dipped beams lighting up the tarmac ahead and filling us with expectation.

'Bet you this is them,' one of us would say when we heard a car slow, our excitement barely containable, a communal giddiness that sometimes caused small accidents. Invariably it wasn't you; Dad drove very slowly and falteringly in his Fiat 131 and was so hard on the gears that you could hear them crunch as he advanced.

'They're here, they're here!' But, again, you weren't, and we would watch with waning energy, drawing shapes in the condensation of our breath, until it was dark and we could see the reflections of our small, hope-filled faces in the glass.

And now you are coming towards me. You haven't seen me yet – your head is down and you're dragging a black bin along the gravel path, leaving deep ridges in its wake. As you get closer I feel that old burgeoning anticipation. I know you can't hear me with the noise of the bin and through the double-glazed window, but I still call out to you. You will be irritated by my being here first, for having forgotten some part of our arrangement. And when you see me you will detect the relief in my face and my voice that you are home and that you are safe, resenting the unspoken pressure I am putting on you to stay healthy and with us and alive.

At the very last moment – I can even hear you tease the key in the lock – something unseen makes you turn around. And now you are walking away from me, back down the garden path, out the front gate, on down the road and out of view.

One

Face: symmetric, properly placed eyes, skin with red-violaceous mortem lividity in its entirety, with large amounts of sand.

'Mum?'

Nothing.

'Mum?' Louder, more strident.

'Sorry, sorry,' you'd say and rub the film of saliva on your lips with the knuckle of a finger. You'd hoist yourself upright, recross your slippered feet and squint at the television with a puzzled frown.

Soon your head would begin to droop again and your blinking would slow. Your expression would be one of intense concentration – you would try your best to stay awake but it was always a fight you would lose. With a final sharp jolt – a hangman's noose – you'd be gone, sleep would have won and you would no longer hear your child calling you.

'Mum?' I'd say again, but I'd get no response so I would give your arm a tentative nudge. 'Mum, you're snoring,' I'd whine, irritated by your unreachableness, doing all I could to deny you that delicious, impossible-to-recreate-in-bed sleep. Why would no one ever allow your small, raw, exhausted eyes to rest when you had been awake for so much longer than anyone else?

'Gosh, I've been up for hours!' you'd say in the mornings. Bright and competitive, walking shoes on, the cold air you'd brought with you billowing all over our sleep-stale breath, you would list everything you'd already achieved while your husband and children were still horizontal. Sleep was an indulgence to you, sleep deprivation your badge of honour, worry your nocturnal activity, your dark secret.

In sleep, your eyes moved rapidly beneath their thin, blue-veined lids, trying to solve the myriad of problems you'd suppressed in your waking hours. You were always expecting some sort of disturbance, something to be attended to that you alone had the duty and the ability to successfully deal with. It could be that ruddy leak in the attic that nearly caused the hall ceiling to collapse last time, or the jolting ring of the doorbell in the small hours revealing a drunken teenage daughter who'd forgotten her keys again, or one of the remarkably poorly chosen tenants of the basement flat who kept locking themselves out. 'Being a landlord has its drawbacks as well as its privileges,' you'd said to Dad as you clambered back into the warmth of bed one winter's night, having supplied the tenant with the spare key to their abode. It had made him laugh so unexpectedly and so uproariously that you couldn't help but giggle a little yourself in the darkness, as you tried to get comfortable again – and he'd repeated the story at parties many times. He always found you most amusing when you weren't trying to be funny.

When sleep finally came, it would be fitful and shallow and any possibility of deeper slumber would be abandoned before the first shipping news on Radio 1. When you'd open the curtains on another day, you would never admit to tiredness, though it always showed in your eyes. The lid of your weaker one, the right, would begin to droop; the eye itself swivelling ever so slightly towards your nose, your lazy eye becoming more pronounced as the day proceeded.

Your eyes were never 'properly placed'; one was always half-watching your children or trained towards your husband, trying to catch his reaction, to see if he found whatever it was on TV as interesting, shocking or funny as you did. 'It's just so silly,' you'd say, weeping with laughter and rubbing your eyes. They would irritate you most in the evenings, not just from weariness but from worries about money, and a possible allergic reaction to your new expensive Lancôme moisturiser that promised to banish signs of fatigue, but instead left your eyes puffy and sore.

*

Light, kettle, radio, oven – you animated everything on entering a room, humming happily as you pottered about the small, sauna-like kitchen that was your domain. Your draw was magnetic and we descended, surrounded and attached ourselves to you, blood-hungry leeches sucking out everything vital: Tayto and pink ham, help with homework, your soft, healing hugs. Soon the kitchen would be too hot and too full of humans who needed your attention but we would go on taking till we were swollen and sated and you were entirely spent.

'It's like an oven in here,' you'd say, as you clattered about cupboards for the saucepan you needed, bent low, your dress rising up at the back to expose your thighs in tan tights. Your ceaseless humming would take on a more manic edge as you became increasingly addled. You were profoundly uncomfortable in silence, needing to fill it with words or with humming; you hummed tunelessly all the time.

You'd stretch over the sink to yank open the sash window behind the kitchen curtain – the fan built into its pane was broken and useless, covered in black masking tape and gunk and grease. An imprint of this window in miniature would remain etched on your eyeball as you turned back to a boiling pot. The image slid, oil-slick, down your cornea and shot up again when you blinked, infiltrating everything until it dissipated.

As your internal temperature rose, it would cause your rosacea to flare and spread across your nose and cheeks, and your face would flush from standing upright too swiftly. Beads of sweat would dot your upper lip and patches of damp would darken your armpits.

Sometimes, like a neglected pot on the hob, you would boil over. You would bite down hard on your lower lip as you gave the kitchen door an almighty slam. 'Dash it! Damn it! For crying out loud!' This startled and silenced everyone, not only because these moments were rare but because to us they seemed entirely unpredictable. We always failed to spot the warning signs, and when you snapped it was invariably over seemingly trivial things, like the crème caramel you made once: you very skilfully slid a plate under the mould, then turned it over – careful, careful – so that the set pudding would be displayed in all its patterned splendour. We all held our breath as you lifted the plastic mould to reveal the crème caramel, which immediately collapsed into a gelatinous heap and slid, jellyfish-like, into the sink.

*

You'd never been fond of looking people in the eye. Often, whole evenings would pass without you ever making direct visual contact with the person you were talking to, or you'd lock your gaze on someone entirely separate from the conversation, so much so that that person would eventually be forced to look away to break the intensity of your stare.

You'd squeeze your eyes shut at bad news, as if that would make it somehow not true, and also when you were waiting for someone to hurry up and finish their point so that you could get on with your more interesting one. You'd close them too for tiny power naps between jobs, to manage your exhaustion, like that woman who sailed solo around the world.

You told me a thousand times ('Ah pet, I've told you a thousand times!') but I still can't remember how you singed off all of your eyelashes. You'd look at me sidelong in the car with some envy as I'd apply more mascara to my already stiff and congealed ones. I'd have ballyragged you into giving me a lift into town and you'd shoot your hand out instinctively to protect me whenever you had to stop suddenly, which was quite often because you were never fully focused on the road ahead.

Your eyes were blue, like mine – little b little b, homozygous recessive – but they were a paler, more apologetic hue: ballet blue, the blue of the Virgin Mary statue that lay decapitated on the shelf above my bed for all of my childhood. Not the piercing, cobalt blue of some of your children – or perhaps your eyes began vividly blue and faded, the way age fades everything.

Blue is your colour. Sky blue, aqua blue, cyan blue – like shallow water on a sandy beach. *Large amounts of sand.* Large amounts of sand in the collapsing dunes we charged down at Brittas Bay, you always behind us like a weary Sherpa burdened with belongings – picnic basket, blankets, buckets and spades – pausing between spiky tufts of marram grass above where we rolled and plunged to seek out a sheltered spot on the beach.

You'd sit wide-legged on the picnic blanket, like a doll whose legs have to be splayed to make it sit upright, as you organised and unpacked, your legs a solid ballast against the breeze, a way to keep the blanket from flapping up and turning in on itself, covering the items that we needed.

Large amounts of sand in my sandwich. 'Oh, pet, it's perfectly fine,' you would say, brushing your fingers over its Easi Single centre while I cried that you'd just made it sandier and your eyes searched for the bag for rubbish. Grains of sand got everywhere: in the curves of our ears, in the cracked ridges of our lips, between our toes and bum cheeks, in the lengths of our sea-soaked hair.

*

When the wave came, did the sand storm and needle your lashless eyes? Were they open, wild and startled, as the great crash of the silt came down on top of you and plunged you into a sealed submarine world? Or did you squeeze them shut when you went under? Were you wearing snorkelling goggles? Did they pull the skin around your eyes and stretch them narrow? Were your blinking eyes trapped behind that mask, looking blindly for help?

Did you feel real terror in those moments after you lost your footing and cut your head and when the aneurysm charged, tsunami-like, through vessels and veins? Was there a moment of realisation? A second of acceptance? Or only frantic grappling and panic, silent screams, violently flailing limbs as the waves forced you under again and again, each time you tried to surface?

Perhaps you didn't struggle at all. Perhaps you simply let go, surrendered, relaxed. Perhaps for the first time in your life you did something entirely selfish. You let go and closed your eyes because you were seventy-two and so very tired. Perhaps you let your heavy, grit-filled, blue eyes close and finally rest.

Two

Mouth: closed lips with violaceous mortem lividity.

Ears: properly placed, with large amounts of sand and red-violaceous mortem lividity.

Something happened to your second-eldest son when he returned to Boston after your burial: his voice changed. For more than two weeks he could speak only in a whisper. His family could barely hear him; they asked him to repeat himself and to please talk a little louder, but he was unable to. It was as though he were afraid that if he raised his voice he might wake someone.

'Why can't you speak like your mother?' had been Dad's lifelong rhetorical question to us. So sensitive to others' accents, timbres and intonations, he found your speaking voice flawless and badgered all of his children to emulate it. 'Silvery' was how the parish priest described it at your funeral service, the word itself slicing bright through echoing coughs and reverberating bells in the full church.

Father C was familiar with the sound of your voice because you did the second reading at Mass every other Sunday, each word carried so crisp and clean that there was little need for the microphone that he fiddled with and adjusted for others. Reading read, you would descend the carpeted steps of the altar, pious and serious, as though setting an example for the rest of the congregation. You retook your seat in the pew beside your adult daughter – me – who tried even then to get your attention, pointing out a possible neighbour, whispering a request for a mint. In church I was an eternal child, tracing fingers around the initials of the dead on brass plaques, distracted by swollen ankles spilling over the high shoes of the aged with their dandruff-flecked winter coats and freckled bald pates, fighting the urge to pivot to look at the choir in the gallery or a screaming toddler carried away in her father's arms. Let us pray. And down you went, further out of reach, sinking your face in your hands and reeling off prayers so familiar that they had lost all meaning.

Though it was the setting of many auspicious family occasions – baptisms, confirmations and marriages – a sense of death always hung heavy in our parish church: in the wine-coloured curtains of the confessional boxes, in the hollow of the ringing bell, in the incense rising from the thurible swung by a priest in purple, in the elderly parishioners' increasingly unpredictable bodies, like that poor woman in the floral dress who sat on the step of the side entrance one day, head bowed and clinging to her handbag, while urine flowed from her in a swift narrow stream along the tarmacadam.

It wasn't just death that any thought of that church brought to mind, but those other enduring emotions of a Catholic upbringing: guilt and shame. Shame when I burst out of the First Communion dress inherited from my slimmer sister, being somewhat protuberant of tummy even at eight. Or 'stout', as Granny would have said, that one short word instantly summoning a detailed memory of her.

On another occasion I, along with others considered to possess the best voices in the class, had been selected to sing at the altar of a sombre school-centenary Mass. You were there somewhere in the crowd of parents, sitting upright and pigeon-chested with pride. Our music teacher, high up in the gallery on her organ, began the opening chords of a well-rehearsed hymn an octave too high, giving our voices nowhere to go by the chorus, which resulted in the most ferocious attack of rib-aching giggles that could not be subdued for the remainder of the service. The deeper the trouble we were in (and the violent prodding from our livid teachers in the row behind us as we retook our seats after each destroyed hymn told us it was pretty damn deep), the more impossible the giggles were to quell.

*

We could never detect the apparently stark differences between our accents and yours that so incensed our father and caused him to snort with exasperation. He corrected my nasal drawl before I could ever finish a sentence, but I didn't know how to move my muffled words from the back of my throat to the front edge of my teeth, how to free them from my permanently clogged sinuses so I could enunciate crisply and clearly from the tip of my tongue.

Decades later, before the ear, nose and throat consultant had even taken out his needle-thin camera to peer up my nose, he said I sounded miserable. He asked if I'd ever sustained a nasal injury – and in that moment, a memory formed of me sitting on the granite gate pillar of the Swiss embassy, aged nine or ten, trying to summon the courage to jump to the ground as an initiation into some gang of local kids. I misjudged it, panicked after I leapt, changed my mind mid-freefall and hit the concrete path hard, face first. I cut my lip and whacked my nose, causing my septum to deviate badly and blocking all the turbinates around it – neither of which I or you or Dad ever noticed; I didn't know noses even had turbinates. Two surgeries later, I'm still learning how to breathe and to speak in the way that you spoke.

You would never not answer the phone. Even four floors up in the old house, you would take off at speed down the stairs if the phone rang, humming as always but on these occasions producing a different sound, a sort of *ay-yi-yi*, to let your snoozing, indifferent family know that, as swiftly as you were travelling, you might not reach it in time. If you had company or were in the middle of making dinner, you'd still charge to pick it up before the answerphone clicked in. After you'd said hello, there'd be a subtle shift in the cadence of your voice to match the accent and attitude of the caller, but before long you'd become impatient with whoever it was and would start to shake the receiver, holding it ever further from your ear, to hurry them up because you had so many other things to do.

Although you were the only one who ever answered (even the receiver of the grubby beige phone smelt of you, milky and intimate), while Dad was alive and with five children in the house, the calls were rarely for you. Sometimes it was a local constituent, for instance the elderly widow of an army officer, who would spend a long time telling you what needed to be done to the country as Dad stood in the background, providing a running commentary in a loud whisper for you to interpret and pass on. Sometimes it was his best friend, just to tell him a joke. ('Is your Papa there?' he would ask if any of us answered, making Dad sound like an entirely different father from the one that was ours.) Then you would pass over the phone and listen in while attempting to load the dishwasher without making any noise, and although you could hear only one side of their conversation, you couldn't help but chuckle along with his laughter.

In those years you had no time to form friendships of your own, as you admitted yourself in a tearful fury after one of your less successful dinner parties. There'd been a power cut while the Ballymaloe bread was baking, leaving it soggy at the centre and inedible, and another politician's wife had sat on Dad's lap at dessert while you cleared the table to make room for your profiterole tower.

When all of us were gone and the silence – the five seconds of peace you had forever pleaded for and craved – was finally yours, you were at a loss. It was such a novel, discombobulating sensation that you had to fill it, colour it in, with the TV and with the phone, now set on the old coal bucket beside you in the evenings so you didn't have to dash to the kitchen to pick it up when it rang. During calls you'd consult your diary, a black, pocket-sized one of the type Dad had bought you for Christmas each year to keep on top of parties and appointments, and you'd swiftly fill up all the hours-days-weeks-months and years of your life; every rectangle scribbled in with busy-ness and responsibility.

As you worked, you'd sometimes send the top of your pen to explore the whorl of your ear, probing your ear canal between entries and inspecting it for wax when you pulled it out again. Was I ever not watching you? Invading even these tiny, private moments – how unfair to observe someone when they don't know they are being watched and possibly seeing things they don't especially want you to see. Sitting on the stairs, my face wedged between the slats of the bannisters, or draped perilously over them, I was watching, watching you always.

*

Closed lips with violaceous mortem lividity. Violaceous means of a violet colour. Violet was one of your colours. Your mouth was rarely closed, even in sleep, and your tongue never lay still: it glided along your teeth, explored your molars, hit against your soft palate. Over the years, you developed a cough from your blood pressure medication and from food that kept getting in the way of your words. 'It's just a crumb,' you always said, irritated by our concern, your face turning the colour of the beetroot in your salad and your eyes watering from congestion. And you often had a bubble in your throat, a thick, phlegmy sound that gave a small echo to what you were saying and became quickly intolerable to your children, who demanded that you cough some more to clear it.

I had been furious with you the morning your teeth fell out onto the kitchen table. You'd been mid-sentence in a story you were telling my big brother and the rest of his band, who'd just arrived off the car ferry from Holyhead in their dirty white tour van. They were hunched around our ship's cabin of a kitchen in second-hand leather jackets, with charcoal-rimmed eyes and cold cigarette breath, and made you, who already looked soft to me, seem vulnerable and exposed. Your eyes were raw and weeping from the smoky grill where sausages, rashers and black pudding were spitting and spluttering and which you would use again at lunchtime to cook Dad two pieces of liver or some pork chops.

Everyone was watching when out with your words, at the crux of your story, came a flesh-coloured, plastic bridge and four false front teeth. They sat on the table/door like a blurted-out truth. My brother, unable to look, squeezed his eyes shut and asked if you were all right. Without teeth, you could only nod in response; you squeezed your own eyes shut too as you fumbled with the slippery bridge and tried to slot it back into place on your palate. I was furious with you for appearing fragile, hating that it had to happen in front of the drummer, whom I had a crush on and who was still digging his spoon deep into the sugar bowl when I got up and left. To see you falter, a mother so unflappable, so cheerfully capable even when cooking dinner for sixty constituents while simultaneously minding your five children, was startling because it was so rare; unsettling because even as young adults we all still depended so heavily on you.

When you sold our old house (before the property bubble burst, accepting the first offer you received, saying you didn't want to be greedy) you didn't have to worry about money for the first time in your adult life. You treated yourself to a new set of teeth. They had always caused you trouble, and you silently suffered aches in your molars so painful and debilitating that we were ordered to leave you alone whenever you were inflicted with one, holding the palm of your hand protectively over the area that hurt, your pallor waxy, your expression defensive and wary. Your new teeth were brilliantly white, disconcertingly uniform and longer than your original ones. They gave you a new, different smile – leporine – and took a while to settle in to your face.

You used to speak deliberately loudly in crowds and though you were ostensibly talking to me, it was the strangers around us you were hoping to amuse with recognition of that comic demonstration of our mother–daughter dynamic. The only times your voice was silenced were when you had one of your toothaches or when other women gossiped and bitched: you were resolutely mute when others were critical. You were diplomatic and non-confrontational, and you didn't do bad news. 'He's dead, unfortunately, but he's in very good form,' Dad said once, impersonating you, your resolute optimism.

'It's OK, Dula,' you used to say, using my baby name and trying to silence me more than comfort my upset, rubbing my back a little too vigorously. 'It'll be fine. Honestly, honestly.' I feel it now too as a mother, the surge of intense irritation when my child falls, the unexpected numbness and robotic calm that takes over in an emergency, because I/you can't/couldn't allow myself/yourself to feel too much.

The other night you turned up in a dream, at the door of a modern glass-fronted house that didn't belong to me and that I should not have been in. I saw you from the lamplit window with women I didn't recognise on either side of you. You were bald and thin and silent. I understood that these women were bringing you to me so that I could take care of you. No words were exchanged between us and soon the others evaporated. I carried you to the bathroom and put you in the sink. You had shrunk to the size of a newborn baby and I washed you with warm water.

*

'Delphine's in trouble!' Did you hear those words, shouted by one of your friends? Did you try to respond and reassure even then, spitting out the rubber mouthpiece of the snorkel, salt water surging up your nose and down the back of your throat, sand funnelling into your ears? Did you feel the swell and sense the spread of panic on the beach? Did you admonish yourself when the crashing wave caused you to lose your footing (already unstable in flippers) and fall backwards and under? 'Ah, Del!' did you say? Or did you apologise, sorry, sorry, your words useless and sealed?

When you surfaced, they said, there was foam at the corner of your mouth. Somebody shouted 'Doctor! Oxygen! Emergency!' while your face turned from deep red to purple.

I see the dark wet patch in the sand where they had set you down, a motionless sand angel. Someone surely brought water – an elixir and a cure for all, even when there was no hope. Were you turned onto your side into recovery position? Did someone prop a T-shirt or a rolled towel under your head?

Was everything around you in motion, while you alone lay still? Were people running along the sand towards you, or away from you to get help? Were others staggering through the sea to reach the shore? Perhaps some of the group were still happily snorkelling, goggled eyes gazing in fascination at the darting bluefish, yellowtail, blackfish, unaware of what was happening just above the surface.

What did the animals do in the commotion? The mockingbirds, the sea lions? Did tourists gather in a crowd around you, with futile offers of help and advice, feeding greedily on the unfolding drama? A scene as primal and as intimate as the moment of birth, witnessed by strangers who would now have the moment of your death forever imprinted in their brains. A private event that should have been for our eyes alone, for those who knew you and who loved you. Walk on, I want to say. Look away, this is none of your business. They eventually got on with their day and the women got back onto the ship. Drama over, protagonist dead.

You would have been deeply embarrassed by all the fuss, irritated that you weren't in a position to take control of the chaos, to calm everyone down as you always did in a crisis. You always knew the next best thing to do.

I see the darkening skies of evening's approach. The incoming tide washing away the last traces of your imprint in the sand, until all the powdered white silica had turned to densely packed brown. Someone told me that the medical staff laughed and joked on board the cruise ship as it pulled out of the bay, that they took photos of the wildlife, that they were chewing gum.

Three

Head dissection: the haematoma of the third middle of the parietal only covers the scalp with its punctiform wound, it does not affect the bone. Brain tissue shows no lesions or collections.

Mum is a Middle English word meaning 'silent'. It may be derived from mummer, one who acts without speaking in a traditional masked mime or a mummers' play. Mum's the word. 'Mum' is the word that was never not said, the one spoken more than any other. Those three letters infiltrated and interrupted your every thought and task. Sometimes you responded to them wearily when no one had called you at all. Even with your ears underwater, even with the blender whirring, the clothes tumbling, car horn sounding, even through your own endless hum, the word was always there, hanging oppressively in the air and demanding an immediate response. As a mother myself, I hear it now too so endlessly that I answer 'yes' out of instinct, sometimes to a child shouting for an entirely different mum.

It was often spoken with slight irritation and the rising intonation of a question. Sometimes a querulous child would give it two syllables: Mu-um? It's the name you taught us to call you, the very first word we spoke as babies – even your grandchildren called you 'Mum' at first, because it was what they heard everyone else call you – but hearing it made you feel sometimes that you were being pulled repeatedly underwater when you were simply trying to swim.

Mum is a valid word in Scrabble: mum is worth seven points. Mum is the word that most clearly defined you to us pre- and post-mortem, that instantly summoned the memory of you to mind, along with optimistic, unflappable, kind, resourceful and addled. Addled, as an adjective, means unable to think clearly – 'I can't hear myself think,' you said often though no one was listening. To addle is to bewilder, perplex, stupefy, exhaust, overcome or occasionally to pester. Addled is worth nine points in a game of Scrabble.

Scrabble was your favourite game; you were good with words. You had a broad vocabulary from a lifetime of reading blockbusters – invariably (another of your words) by Maeve Binchy and only ever in bed or on holidays. Your brain tissue showed no lesions or collections. Just constant interruptions and things that you alone could put right: blocked drains, burst pipes, punctured tyres, full bins, empty fridges, airlocks, wet beds, nit-riddled kids, knots of slime-covered hair clogging up the plughole in the bathroom.

*

Annie Ernaux writes in *The Years* about how losing a loved one's voice is the worst thing about death, but that using their words somehow brings it back in the exact pitch, cadence and tone.

Your mother's words – ghastly, stout, beastly – were ones that you inherited and ones that I use now; words that have endured through whole generations. These are your words: when I say them aloud, your voice is once again in my head. The other day I described my child's behaviour as beastly, not even ironically. And there you were again, talking through me, and I unconsciously adopting your idiolect as my daughter will one day do with mine.

When making a plan of any sort you would always end it with (DV) (short for *Deo volente*, or God willing). 'When you pass your leaving cert (DV).' 'When we land in Ecuador (DV).' You would also occasionally revert to the Irish '*ar eagla na heagla*', which literally means for fear of fear, or put more simply, 'just in case something goes wrong'.

You weren't a great quoter, though you did have certain P. G. Wodehouse stories, the one about the prize-giving at Market Snodsbury Grammar School, for instance, very fresh in your memory. You always described a particular person's face as 'sad in repose' and a friend's daughter as 'great! Big and bouncy!'

There was a poem you used to recite the first few lines of, about the River Arno, that one of the nuns at school taught you. I can't find any references to it online and none of my siblings recall it and so it is gone now for good.

One evening while searching for some lost thing, I found a small padlocked diary from when you were twenty – the key forever lost, allowing unbridled access to you. And you are there, fully animated again, in the words I can decipher; your handwriting was rushed and slanted even then, as though you were permanently running late:

Had a rather complicated journey home and for some unknown reason bought myself a pink hat.

Wasted a lot of time but felt awfully satisfied with myself.

Began to think about getting down to work but don't imagine it had a positive effect.

Latin paper ghastly as always but then if you don't know any Latin it is bound to be.

We were making a ferocious racket, a whale of a racket, an almighty racket …

And you are right beside me again after so many years, though it is an earlier version of yourself, long before you ever had children; before we had ever met, yet still undeniably, irrefutably you.

*

Some friends called their parents by their Christian names, but you were never Delphine to your children. Delphine was a different person, someone we hadn't met. A small girl with weak eyes and hair so blonde it was almost white, who existed only in old photographs, running down the gravel laneway in Glengarriff as far as the postbox in a school pinafore, white ankle socks and scuffed sandals, your father timing her as she went. Delphine means dolphin. Your name is derived from the Latin *delphinus*, which in turn comes from the Ancient Greek meaning 'a womb, a fish with a womb, a dolphin'.

When you got married, the person who was Delphine was put away like a matryoshka doll of identities, nested within other dolls of increasing size and detail, placed one inside another, concealed beneath all of your other, busier selves. Beneath the politician's wife, the mother, cook, cleaner, ironer, driver, diplomat – there was Delphine: the smallest, simplest, unadorned doll, the one that couldn't be opened up or split in two.

You would address yourself by name, invariably in frustration or reproach. 'Ah, Del!' you scolded yourself, addled as you ferried Dad's lunch of liver, onion gravy and potatoes on the red tray (Dad is valid in Scrabble too but it's only worth five points) because you'd forgotten some condiment. You turned the knob of the study door in silence and with skill, so as not to disrupt him while he read.

Balancing the red tray as you opened the door was a perilous task. There was always the very real risk of upending the lot, sending the grilled liver, like a bloody afterbirth, sliding off the plate and slapping onto the hall carpet, hot gravy splashing ugly greasy streaks over the huge Persian rug that Dad had decided, with pride, to hang on the wall (we watched, bemused) rather than lay across the floor. Another thing in our home that was something it was not, like the kitchen table/door.

The trick was to hoist your right knee high beneath the tray and to move your ringed hand and splay your fingers along its base, under the plate. But it was hottest here and the heat made you angry; you bit down hard on your lower lip as now you carried the tray into and across the room with careful concentration. You safely secured it on the table beside the standard lamp while your husband read in calm, soft, lamplit order, his focused brain able to soundproof itself from the feral, whining, needy, Mum-calling horde on the other side of the door.

Occasionally he would emerge, hunger forcing him from his work, to get the ruddy tray himself. (Ruddy. Another of your words. Whenever you were very cross you'd use it as your expletive of choice – your own mother used it too – it was probably the rudest word I ever heard you say.) You really are the ruddy limit! And we would scatter and hide, like mice along the skirting boards, because of some rule we were infringing.

Dad had mastered the knee-balancing trick too, as he'd back out of the kitchen with the same tray, using his slippered foot to close the door against his arguing children and loquacious mother-in-law, our adored granny, who lived in the basement for several years and who bowed her head ever so slightly in his presence and addressed him only as 'Mr Kelly'.

When I think of my father he is always framed, forever on a threshold: in a black-and-white photograph or by a door – the hall door, shooing away my stray cats (eleven of them at one stage – I provided shelter and food for them in the garden shed) with his heavy tan brogues; on the threshold of the kitchen door, red-faced, telling us his best friend had died; at my bedroom door wet-eyed with affection, holding his wireless; or at the table/door in his Aran jumper eating his cream crackers and Bovril. Forever in a liminal space between the past and the present. Liminal – occupying a position at, or on both sides of, a boundary or threshold. Dad was always backing out of the room, always retreating and leaving us to go somewhere else.

While sorting through some boxes recently, I found a small newspaper cutting. It's a photograph of Dad taken from behind. He is wearing his grey tweed suit, his hands plunged deep into his trouser pockets so that the vent of his suit jacket is pulled up like an inverted V. He is standing at a window, balding head slightly bowed. The caption read thus:

> *An astonishing number of readers failed to identify the rear side of Fine Gael's John Kelly in last week's pictorial competition. Many people thought it was Dr Patrick Hillery. However, some of you got it right and especially Marie Mackin of Kingscourt, Co. Cavan. Her winning caption was 'John Kelly reflecting on the seat of power.'*

In contrast to your husband, you moved in a perpetual forward motion: to the phone, to the door, to catch one of us when we were falling, to take a pot off the ring before it boiled over, blurred or looking beyond in every photograph taken of you – unable to ever be still.

So many of your words were verbs of motion: you pottered (in India you saw a cow pottering up and down a train platform), you trotted and repaired (you packed your bags and repaired to the pool), you retired (for the night with a cup of hot milk). You ventured forth, you nipped, popped, or dashed. You pootled quite regularly. You set off for the station armed with a map. And we were always foostering about.

One of your travel journals records that you 'duly arrived and slept intermittently'. 'We arrived at a reasonable hour.' Times of day were always described as being either reasonable – she got home at a reasonable hour – or ungodly: 'I got home at an ungodly hour.'

After Dad's death, the study became your retreat. You sat with small snacks of figs and prunes and wrote essays for the various diplomas and degrees that you took on with gusto as a widow. Your essays, like your speech, were long, rushed streams of thoughts and ideas, without any punctuation and occasionally plagiarised. 'Plagiarise!' – something else you liked to randomly recite. 'Plagiarise, plagiarise plagiarise.'

This came, I have discovered, from a song by Tom Lehrer, an American musical comedian of the

1950s and '60s, and was itself a tribute to a song by Danny Kaye, whom I loved as a child and intended to one day marry.

You sought out this solitude, surrounded by your dead husband's books, not just to study but to play solitaire and online Scrabble against faceless and invisible opponents. The main purpose of your personal computer, aside from it helping to keep your mind agile as you aged and the handiness of booking trips on it, was the opportunity to hone your skills against an opponent who knew all the permissible-but-obscure two-letter words.

*

The pearl necklace we chose for you to be buried in had slipped to the side in your coffin and it looked uncomfortably tight around your short and smooth neck. We had imagined you wearing it standing upright, vertical, vital. Another thing I've inherited from you, aside from hypothyroidism, was the habit of stretching the neck of your T-shirt or jumper, nestling your nose beneath it and exhaling warm air over your chest and stomach. My father and his best friend agreed that a long neck in a woman was a sign of beauty. You had a short neck, which I have inherited. Dad most admired women who didn't move their faces too much. Like nuns, he used to say.

*

A punctiform wound sounds like a small, neat injury. Very small but not microscopic. A tiny, targeted thing – the dot of a pencil, the pin-like proboscis of a mosquito, the sharp edge of the kitchen cupboard on which you were forever hitting your forehead when you stood up too swiftly from loading or unloading the dishwasher, never protesting, never asking for or expecting help.

A haematoma is messier – a seeping out of blood from vessels, spreading into the surrounding tissues, burgeoning and more ominous. I had my own haematoma, a subchorionic one, in my second pregnancy. But it wasn't the haematoma that made my baby fold in her tiny limbs and die at seventeen weeks' gestation; her post-mortem said that the blood supply between us had been severed because her umbilical cord was hypercoiled. Her miniscule arms were crossed on her chest when the midwife handed her to me. We had identical frontal veins protruding from the tops of our foreheads to just above our eyebrows. The brutal severance of mother and child had brought them pulsing to the surface beneath our tissue-thin skins.

Her father, Charlie, and I called our lost child Lucia, meaning light. She had tried so hard to stay alive in those months of enforced bed rest and I had tried hard too, perhaps too hard, torn between the need to keep her heart beating and the pain of separation from my robust and bossy four-year-old, who would burst through the door of my hospital room once a week – cerulean blue eyes beneath a wild swirl of champagne-coloured curls – and tumble into my arms, where I would hold her so tight she would soon wriggle to get free. Did I cling on so tight to Lucia that she too had to let go? So tight that her life force was smothered? Sometimes I wonder if we needed you too much. Did we put too much pressure on you to stay alive? To scrabble is to grasp for something in order to collect or hold on to it.

'That's nothing,' a man said to his granddaughter when she asked about a fledgling who had fallen from its nest in the dank underbelly of the bridge beyond the train station in Bray, where rock pigeons thronged in the rafters. The man shoved the tiny bird against the wall with the side of his shoe then stood heavily on it, twisting the toe, crushing its miniature bones, nullifying the very existence of a tiny thing that had barely lived before it died.

*

When not challenging the computer, you played Scrabble with the board positioned precariously on a wicker stool between you and your adored sons home from abroad; I would find long, slanting lists of scores on the backs of coffee-ringed envelopes. You placed an awkward late-game Q beside a convenient I. As every assiduous Scrabble player knows, Q-I spells qi, meaning life force.

Two things happened on the night before you travelled to Gardner Bay in the Galápagos. You were all staying at the resort in little chalets on stilts. An earthquake woke you in the early hours. None of you was scared, just curious. The other women went back to sleep but you and your friend stood on the balcony and chatted to each other through the aftershocks.

That same evening, before bed, before sleep, before that minor earthquake, you lost at Scrabble. Your opponent was 'cock-a-hoop', I was told. One of the women said you had never looked more beautiful than on that night that you lost at your best game; another said your skin was blotchy and that you just didn't seem yourself.

Four

Upper and lower limbs: mortem lividity in their entirety, red-violaceous in their distal points, and pale soles of the feet.

Feet: left hallux lacking the nail bed, with a surgical scar, onychomycosis in nails of fourth and fifth left and right toes, with moderate pallor and zones of light mortem lividity.

Dapper gentlemen drawn by the *Vanity Fair* artist known as Spy were hung at regular intervals on the walls of the stairs. They watched you trudge by, up and down, coming and going umpteen times a day, with porridge and post and clothes baskets and plump, needy children. If these caricatures had become suddenly animated, they would never have trudged, as you did. They would have glided, lean and light-footed, unburdened by any extra baggage or flesh, everything as taut as their thin canes and narrow noses, tight quadriceps making their bony knees crack under creased dress-suit trousers.

You spent thirty years of your life negotiating these stairs till the carpet was threadbare, till the dry timber beneath groaned and squeaked. Dad discouraged us from descending or ascending them at their centre to prevent the 'new' (fifteen-year-old) moss-green carpet from wearing – so we endeavoured to stick to the sides, always in our shoes to save the soles of our socks.

Even when you ate, you were always on the edge of your seat, unable ever to settle or finish a meal. You were immediately up again almost as soon as you had sat down, for something forgotten or requested or to retrieve some sauce or dressing from the cooker or the fridge.

And you walked fast, fast enough to keep up with your whippet-thin husband. Not long before you died you had taken to striding ahead of your grown children, increasingly impatient in a large group, irritated by collective indecisiveness and disorder. You only ever slowed on hills, to catch your breath, sometimes declaring that you hated them, as if the discomfort was the hill's fault alone – you would never admit to finding them hard because you weren't as young or as fit as your companions. You always pretended, hands on hips, tilting slightly back on your heels, that you were pausing simply to admire the view.

You stumbled a lot, as I stumble now. The sight of a falling parent is unsettling in the extreme, though not as unnerving as it is for the adult hurtling through the air as the hard pavement surges towards them.

Then the violent, bone-thudding whack of impact, the mean sting of torn and bleeding skin, the embarrassment, the apologising, the trying not to cry.

Once, you stumbled on the stairs outside the kitchen at a drinks party you were hosting for your neighbours, upending a large bowl of fruit punch on the doctor from number 12 who, after insisting that it was nothing at all and that he was perfectly fine, slipped away as soon as he could to go home and change his sodden shirt.

I think I was the one who caused you to trip that time; I'd distracted you by holding your hand. We never held hands – even as a child I'd clung to your folded elbow instead, like a permanent appendage. I'd offered you the top of my head for a kiss when I arrived and you had pulled me towards your chest momentarily, before encouraging me gently but quite firmly away from you. I could see that your rosacea had flared up and I knew not to demand or expect your undivided or even your divided attention that day. I still don't know why I took your hand – perhaps it was the habit I'd developed of reaching for my own daughter's whenever she was close by – but the intimacy of the gesture had been unsettling for us both.

And you tripped over the mop and bucket on our back stairs the day we were invited to Áras an Uachtaráin to meet President Mary Robinson. It was shortly after Dad had died and you were more addled than usual because my big brother hadn't come home from a night out (already in his twenties, it was irritation at his tardiness rather than concern for his safety that most irked you). All I remember of that day, aside from your fall, was the knuckle-whitening drive down the quays to the Phoenix Park, and that the pocket of the president's suit jacket was torn.

You regularly stubbed your toe, on the leg of the bed or on some other sharp unseen object, causing pain so acute that it rendered you speechless for a few seconds. *Left hallux lacking the nail bed.* (A hallux is a person's big toe or the innermost digit of the hind foot of vertebrates.) You used to cut a V-shape in the middle of each of your toenails to encourage them to grow in that direction rather than curling around the sides. You told your children to do the same, cautioning us that ingrown toenails were hereditary. So all the Kelly toes had small Vs cut in to their nails, as some lucky lobsters have cut into their tails, allowing them to be freed by fishermen from their rusted pots and tossed back into the sea to breed.

Despite this encouragement, your left big toenail persisted in retreating painfully into your skin and finally the sensation was so intolerable that you had to have it surgically removed. When we visited you – a scruffy gaggle of small geese, we were – your nail-less toe was concealed in a metal box beneath a sun-warmed yellow hospital blanket, like a caged bird or a surprise to be revealed. We were not allowed to see it or to touch it. It was a positive thing though, this removal of the nail, this repair of our mother, now without a tiny part of her. We didn't feel repulsed by it, or even very curious of the cicatrice that remained; rather, it was an added source of comfort, being undeniably the nail-less toe of the foot of the leg that belonged and led to the rest of you.

You never concealed this flaw from us and on even a vaguely sunny day you would expose it, your toe peeping out of your white Scholl sandals, as round and shiny as an acorn. Exposure seemed to be somehow beneficial – sunlight aided its healing. And there the toenail was not, as though it had never been, at the end of your tanned and hair-free legs, spread out in another V-shape on the picnic rug in the garden, your lemon-coloured skirt flattened between them for modesty.

The front of the toe was a snaggle of stitches that looked like the garibaldi squashed-fly biscuits Granny used to buy us from the Wee Stores. It faded into a squinting sort of scar that sometimes appeared to me like a winking eye or, when it was trapped beneath tan tights, a tiny gurning terrorist, toes bunched fleshily together, fused like Barbie doll ones.

In the tedium of the long summer holidays, I'd sausage-roll myself up in the blue picnic blanket and happily study this newly nail-less toe. Then I would seek out the nettle-rash pattern on the inner side of your knees, a cluster of tiny white pimples encircled in red, like the ones on the chicken you basted with butter and stuffed with breadcrumbs for Sunday lunch, and sometimes question you about it. 'I'm not sure, pet, from sitting too close to the heater,' you'd say, considering it briefly yourself while keeping your little finger on the paragraph of your book to mark the place you very much hoped to return to. 'No, they're not sore, no, not stings.' The term you weren't looking for is erythema ab igne, also known as hot-water bottle rash, a skin condition caused by long-term exposure to heat. I have the same rash on the bulge of my inner knees now, which serves me right, in a way. (Like the time I teased my sister about having her period while needing the bathroom myself only to discover that I was also now bleeding from downstairs.)

Did the mortem lividity cover it too, that nettle-rash skin on the insides of your knees? (*Mortem lividity*. Two deadly, angry words. Dad running up the stairs livid; me running faster, fearing mortem.) A dark-blue staining of the dependent surface of a cadaver, due to the pooling of blood.

And I would go on plainly studying different parts of you, entirely happy in that moment because you were beside me and you were still, like the heavy-trunked wasp that was sucking sugar from the edge of my glass of Ribena: needle needle needle, it went, on its spindly legs as it ingested. It would move soon, though you would go first.

Where am I in this picture? I can't see myself, only you in relation to me. I was always waiting for you, watching you. As a teenager I considered you with faint contempt, sulking, fulminating against some terrible injustice concerning food or money or freedom and what my siblings had been given or allowed compared to me. When I cried you would pat my back, always a little too vigorously, endeavouring to both soothe and silence me.

Where were you looking while I indulgently examined your imperfections and flaws? Shaking your hair back off your face, squinting skyward? 'Glorious,' you'd say on sunny days, and then catch something in your peripheral vision that would irritate you into action – roses that needed deadheading, maybe – or remember a sudden need for a trip to the butcher's for chops for tea or to go and get changed for a wretched constituency meeting. And off you would go, picnic blanket draped over one arm, mug of coffee in your hand, your book under your armpit. As transient as the sun when it briefly breaks through and warms the wool of the blanket before being eclipsed for the rest of the day by a thick bank of grey cloud.

*

Distal points are those parts situated away from the centre of the body or from the point of attachment. If you were the point of attachment, was I a distal point? Were each of your five children distal points of attachment? Are you more distal when you're more distant?

Your fingers, those distal points, were often red-tipped and greasy, from smearing butter on a baking tray or stuffing the chicken for Sunday lunch. When you stood in a daze at the kitchen window sipping from a glass of water held in one hand, you would flex and point the other. This pose annoyed me intensely, unfairly and irrationally, especially as I'm always at a loss as to what to do with my spare hand too. The distal point of your foot as you eyed yourself in the mirror – that private pose we all instinctively adopt when seeing our mirror image – was another part of your ballerina stance. Did you see me behind you in the reflection? Always, always watching you, even when you were simply wondering what on earth to wear that evening, for pity's sake, my hands a small-scale simulacrum of yours.

At your aqua-aerobics classes, you would lower yourself gingerly down the chrome ladder into the swimming pool. Without your Scholl sandals, your nail-less toe was naked and defenceless and you had gashed it getting into a pool one summer. A surgical scar. The old scar from your ingrown toenail operation had left your leg vulnerable to infection and its circulation poor; it led to recurring episodes of cellulitis, the bacteria entering your system through that tiny orifice or from a small nick you had given it as you got in or out of the water. Those little wounds healed slowly and the bacteria stagnated, causing what began as a small infection to become a systemic one.

The cellulitis was a creeping redness, a danger making itself known. A whisper from the universe that all was not well. These tumbles and minor illnesses, as well as the ever-increasing trips abroad, seemed to act as little warnings and practice runs – small strokes, minor quakes – to help us get used to the idea of losing you. Your leg became glossy red, hot and tender and painful. For several weeks as I walked on my routine way, I would chant a mantra: 'My mother is wonderfully healthy and well.' While you sat, furious at being kept from your regular commitments, with one leg up on the wicker stool in your small sitting room. An ankle sock like a child's, brilliant white against the livid skin that was shiny as a burn and entirely hair-free.

A memory: we were in Termini station, Rome, in torpid mid-afternoon Italian heat, my daughter and I, several years after your death. Everything was in motion: commuters and tourists rushing or lost, shouting, announcements over the tannoy. We were waiting, with all of our bags, at the first platform – *binario uno* – for a train that would take us to Terontola, Cortona.

An intercity train had nudged its way noisily into the platform in front of us and screeched dryly to a halt, emitting a deep exhale. An elegant elderly woman made a tremulous and careful descent down the steel steps and hopped rigidly over the significant gap between the train and the platform, landed with a relieved look on to terra firma and turned to wait for her friend to disembark. The second woman missed her footing as she stepped off and her front leg plunged deep into the gap. She cried out in shock and pain and several onlookers rushed to hoist her up from where she was now sandwiched. Her leg had caught against some part of the train's mechanism as she was being lifted and flesh was stripped from the bone so that when her leg was exposed again, it hung in strips like meaty curtains all the way up to her knee. On seeing her injury – shock must have numbed the pain – and the horrified expressions of onlookers, the woman began to cry and stood at a loss, still holding her bag at the crook of her elbow. And everyone witnessing the scene seemed momentarily stunned into inaction, everyone was still. Then someone shouted for help, someone else was summoned to get a chair.

*

When the group arrived at Española Island on the morning after the earthquake, they did some exploring and took photos of the wildlife. I can see the boat containing all of you making white frothy scars in the choppy water as you approached. Giddy tourists shouting over the roar of the motor and the rush of the sea, greedy for adventure. The oblivious seals on the shore, bleating, burping and moaning in blubbery huddles, pelicans snattering, blue-footed boobies in their only home on the planet, huge, angry red crabs, water thundering and collecting in pools over lichen-covered rocks. And all of you pale-legged tourists in baggy shorts, floppy hats and novelty T-shirts, clambering inelegantly out of the boat assisted by a nimble local. You all try to engage with him and the one member of your group who gets a reaction instantly gains approval from the others for seeming less of a tourist.

You and some of the other women walked the length of the beach. Did you march ahead, your small feet sinking into the warm sand? Were you breathless then, feeling a bit woozy from the boat but not saying anything to anyone? When you returned you put on your snorkelling gear. You thought you looked ridiculous as you posed for a photo that would be your last: restless, looking away, already mentally in the water, then gone from view.

You were in the water about a minute ahead of your snorkelling partner – always ahead, despite her being far younger and despite the large rocks at the shore's edge that were hidden under the swell. As your partner approached the sea, she was shocked that the natural terrain was so dangerous. She remembers tripping over those rocks as she slowly walked into the water. She thought the guides should have warned the group of these dangers.

The only real danger they had highlighted was the possible presence of jellyfish in the sea. Your partner wore a wetsuit, which she had hired. You wore a dark swimsuit with a matching top over it and a black swim cap. You had put on flippers at the water's edge, as was advised. Did they have to give you children's ones? Or did you have to make do with adult-sized ones that were a poor fit for your feet? Is that why you stumbled on the rocks when the wave came? Because you couldn't balance easily with them on? Did the raw sensation of the wet rubber irritate your bad toe as you walked blindly backwards into the ocean?

Five

On her left annular finger she was wearing a wedding ring, which was removed and handed to the police authorities.

When they pulled you from the water, silty grey waves whipping and crashing against your dying body and the limbs of rescuers, flailing in futile attempts to save you but succeeding in keeping you from being swept out to sea (dead was one thing, lost at sea quite another), your organs were closing down swiftly. A seawater-blue rising and spreading, bringing death to each part of you in turn, changing your colour as it moved, a silent seeping beneath your thin skin until it reached your foaming mouth. Realisation spread too, in undulating lines, from the sea to the sand to beyond the bay and across oceans.

They said both your engagement ring and your wedding ring were still on your hand when they manoeuvred your body to the shore and began CPR, but when you were moved from the Galápagos Islands to the port city of Guayaquil on the mainland, where they left you in a refrigerated room, the rings were missing. The tour leader of the *Legend* cruise ship said that your wedding band – which you never took off, not for sea swimming, not for the butter-basting of chickens, not for the wringing-out of woollens, not for the unblocking of sewage-sputtering drains – was being kept by a high-ranking officer on the island.

When the Irish consul in Ecuador contacted this officer to ask about your missing rings, the officer was confused. He said he didn't know anything about them but that he would contact the tour leader himself. After the authorities spent two months trying to locate the rings, your wedding ring was anonymously sent to the consulate. No one ever discovered who sent it or what had happened to it in the interim. The consulate put it on the glass of a photocopier and faxed the page with its image to my sister who signed it to indicate that it was indeed yours, and your wedding ring was finally returned to the family.

Your engagement ring was never found – maybe they were wrong when they said it was still on your hand when you surfaced. Perhaps it's forever wedged deep in the rocky seabed of Gardner Bay, among the coral, sponges and algae, its diamond dulled and grimy. Did the cold of the seawater make your fingers shrink so that one ring slipped off as you fell? Surely not, when you had so often threaded your fingers through the frigid waters of the Irish Sea without ever taking your rings off first. The bones of your hands were small and delicate, like those of your size-three feet, but extra flesh around your knuckles had kept your rings safely wedged into place for all of your married life.

*

Diary entry: 28 Nov 1960: Officially engaged, very excited.

You told me once as we drove to the bottle bank near Sydney Parade that Dad had asked you to marry him on Sandymount Strand, a long beach near Dublin Port, the tide often so far out that containers and ferries appeared sunken and stuck in the earth along the horizon; further in, swirls of lugworm mounds like walnut whips dotted the hard-packed sand; dogs splashed and chased through sporadic pools of oily water.

14 Jan 1961: Went to Sleeping Beauty with John Kelly.

27 March 1961: John came round for Russian lesson.

Did you at one stage have a Russian flatmate? Perhaps you were taking Russian lessons together? Or perhaps Russian was your code name for something a little more romantic?

28 March 1961: Lots of dashing and rushing and lectures and dress fittings and hair done and plays and suppers and cinemas and visits from Mummy and Daddy and Ray and invitations and material for bridesmaids' dresses and then no time to write after.

*

Your father, Marshall Dudley, is sitting in a wheelchair to your right in one of your framed wedding photographs. He died before meeting any of his grandchildren, at the age of just fifty-eight. The only other photo I've seen of him is the one that had hung forever high on the wall to the left of Granny's bed: he is sitting on horseback, straight-backed and proud in riding jacket, breeches and boots.

Everyone said you adored your daddy. He used to travel to Dublin by train quite regularly when you were studying at Trinity, to take you to Jammet's on Nassau Street for lunch (described by *Vogue* in 1928 as 'one of Europe's best restaurants, crowded with gourmets and wits', where the sole and grouse were 'divine').

Despite the stroke he had suffered before your wedding day, he looks robust in this photograph. It was only when you were pulling out of the driveway of your house, The Garland, with your new husband by your side, that he broke down in tears and could not be consoled. You didn't see him cry – it wasn't in your nature to look back – and no one ever told you how distraught he had been by your departure.

Your mother, Marguerite, moved from Mallow to Dublin sometime after Marshall's death. She lived first near the Wee Stores on Pembroke Lane, and then, when she became less sure of her footing, in the basement flat of our family home, where she spent her last days largely alone, smoking, drinking sherry and watching the races on TV. She would send us to buy her packets of John Player Blue in the shops at the Merrion end of the road, where they never questioned a small dishevelled tomboy asking for such a thing, not caring, I suppose, whether I smoked them myself or passed them to a responsible adult. She taught us to play fish, gin rummy and bridge, offered us Terry's All Gold chocolates and squashed-fly biscuits, and laughed till her laugh became a cackle, then an alarmingly long, phlegm-inducing fit, one gnarled knuckle held – polite yet futile – against her lipsticked, smoker's-lined lips.

You'd been in Belfast, buying her a cassette recorder for Christmas, on the day she died. I worried for a long time that you might have suspected that I killed poor Granny, because I was the one who had found her. I'd dropped down, as usual, to give her a copy of *The Irish Times*, now that Dad had fully ingested its contents at breakfast, along with his porridge and post. When my knocks on her bedroom window were met with no answer, I had let myself in, calling her name in the darkness of the hall, inhaling her scent – tobacco mixed with damp and a dash of 4711 eau de cologne. I knocked again on her bedroom door, finally turning the handle and opening it: a shard of stark morning light had penetrated the thin curtains, illuminating her alabaster face, which was turned to the ceiling. Her eyes were closed, sunken in their sockets, the skin on the lids spider-veined, thin. Her avian, arthritic hands were gripping the salmon-pink blanket with a satin trim, which she had pulled up to just below her chin. Marshall, as ever, was to her left; Jesus on his cross above her head. I called her name a few more times but was too frightened to touch her. Without fully comprehending what I was witnessing, I felt instinctively that I had interrupted a profoundly private, intimate process. I ran upstairs instead to tell my father, knocking hard on his study door, knowing that this was a situation that warranted interrupting his work.

Marshall and Marguerite are buried together in a graveyard in Mallow, County Cork, close to a railway line. At the very moment your mother's body was being lowered into the earth, a train thundered by. Marshall had loved trains all of his life and the timing of this coincidence was a further example to you of the many unexplainable serendipities of life.

The body of a more distant relative, your great-great-great-grandfather, Daniel O'Connell, lies in a crypt beneath a round tower at Glasnevin Cemetery, though his heart is buried in Rome (at Sant'Agata dei Goti, then the chapel of the Irish College), in accordance with his dying wishes.

I only became aware of this connection with 'The Liberator' as an adult, though you had no doubt told me many times when my mind was focused on other important things like boys and clothes and money. I have since learned a little more about him. In addition to freeing the Catholics of Ireland from the Penal Laws, he had campaigned for the abolition of slavery in the United States. He died at the age of seventy-one in May 1847, in Genoa, Italy, of a 'softening of the brain', encephalomalacia.

O'Connell's last years were disappointing and divisive. The greatest blow was the devastation caused by the Great Famine and by that time his health was failing. His voice, which had once dominated enormous meetings and assemblies, became barely audible. Facing death and in low spirits, he set out on a pilgrimage to Rome to receive a blessing from Pope Pius IX. He never reached his destination.

Holes in the marble casing of his coffin allow you to reach in and touch the wood, which is supposed to bring good luck. In a small anteroom next door, several other lead-lined and occupied coffins are piled somewhat unceremoniously in a criss-crossed, horizontal stack: apparently there is space for still one more. Perhaps it will be for one of his many great-great-great-great-grandchildren. At the far end of the same cemetery, in an area called the Angels' Plot, baby Lucia Jewell Whisker is buried close to many other babies who didn't make it. This part of the graveyard is easy to find, crowded as it is with the colours and symbols of childhood – balloons, teddy bears and windmills – but for me it's too painful to visit. A giant of a man (though apparently quite short) and a tiny dead child, both connected by blood to you and to me.

*

Last diary entry:

22 December 1961: Brought John breakfast in bed.

Your fingernails were weak and chipped easily, no matter how much Chivers strawberry jelly you ate. Jelly, you claimed as you tore off a translucent square straight from the packet and sank your teeth into it, would help them become stronger. I liked to remind you, being the virtuous vegetarian that I was, that jelly was made by the boiling of animal skin, tendons, ligaments and bones with water. This neither irritated nor disgusted you; I was a persistent but tolerable background buzz, like the bluebottle fizzing uselessly against the kitchen window, largely ignored until without warning the sound became entirely intolerable and you would fling open the window as wide as you could, tiny chips of dried paint flaking like dandruff as you yanked it with such force to stop the relentless, wretched buzzing in your ears.

It always made you more reflective than it should have done, when your nails snagged and tore. Another of life's umpteen tiny irritations. You would examine the offending article with frustration, your weak eye turning slightly inward towards the bridge of your nose, then suck at the tender, exposed skin beneath. You had a thin, toffee-coloured line just under all of your nail tips, as I now have too, that makes our generally relatively clean nails appear permanently grubby.

Though they were rarely polished, you kept your nails filed short with those powder-covered emery boards I used to steal from your dressing-table drawer from the china box that made a satisfying cupped-closed hollow sound when I replaced its top. Your hands never became knobbly or gnarled like a bird's claw, as happened to your own mother and many other women of similar age. Your hands never grew old.

You used your little finger, rather than your index one, to keep your place in *Mrs Beeton's Book of Household Management* when trying to follow a recipe. Another of your habits which annoyed me enormously, Lord only knows why.

I see your hands in my hands now, when I hold the steering wheel – on the M50 when I feel like I'm just pretending to be a driver while everyone belongs there and knows what they're doing. Yours were always more capable, safer at the helm; those of the sober chauffeur when your husband was a little 'tight'; on trips in the night to collect a homesick child (who examined you forensically and critically even then, even at 2 a.m.). Yours was the hand attached to the arm that shot out to protect whoever was in the passenger seat when you stopped suddenly, though we were wearing seatbelts and were more threatened by the distraction caused by your focus on us than the lack of your superfluous, protective arm. The thumb of your hand that would blanch from being pressed against the windscreen if it was hailing or if loose gravel spilled from a truck ahead. The thousand things you have taught me, never deliberately but acquired indirectly from endless observation, have now become my own habits.

Yours were invariably the hands at the wheel of our Fiat 131 when we went on holidays. The car was an unfashionable, washed-out sort of orange – the same shade as my lookalike Man-from-Atlantis swimming shorts and my aunt's homemade orange ice cream. Dad believed that because Fiats were Italian, they were better equipped to drive us safely up and over and down the other side of 'Thalps', as we called them. You would be the one inching us forward in the queue for the ferry, behind the immeasurably more stylish German and French cars, their rooftop cargo carriers suggesting skiing holidays and glamour. Inevitably, slim, downy-necked, deeply tanned children would turn around to stare solemnly and unapologetically at us. We would see a flowered tissue box or quilted jacket spread across the shelf above the back seat, a jaunty sun hat, and the napes of the beautiful children – never too many, never squished, probably even with a fancy leather arm rest between their slender and sun-kissed limbs. We felt a deep envy for the order and modernity of such a family and I cringed at how old-fashioned mine was: tweed trousers and tortoiseshell glasses, plastic bags of belongings, the stuffy cheese-and-onion-ness of us all.

You were a far more skilled driver than Dad, despite seeming permanently distracted, and would set off blithely and alone with a quarter tank of petrol, an out-of-date map and an absurdly optimistic smattering of foreign currency to drive across the continent. You were optimistic about petrol too and often drove with the needle at empty, abandoning us on the side of the road and trotting off, to use another of your phrases, a red jerry can swinging cheerfully from your hand, in search of a garage to refill it with a fiver's worth of petrol. We never knew that 'filling it up' was even a petrol pump option. Sometimes you took both hands off the steering wheel and waved them wildly in the air in an attempt to alarm your feral brood into silence and conformity.

Dad, on the other hand, was deeply mistrustful of all forms of transportation that weren't running on rails or Shanks's mare, and made halting, faltering progress, avoiding driving whenever walking was an option (he refused a State car as he felt it was a waste of taxpayers' money). He was also fanatical about not wasting petrol. He must have read somewhere that if you push each gear to the maximum, you somehow use less fuel. He would drive along the road, the engine revving to a painfully high pitch, until he finally slipped the clutch and switched gears. He would switch off the engine if stopped at what looked like it might be a long red light, and then start up again when the light went green, turning it off once again on any downhill so that we would freewheel all the way to the nadir.

Dad's hands were very different to yours: tanned, clean, nails with perfect half-moons – *mezzelune* – above his cuticles (a habit of his I've inherited: running my thumbnail along my bottom front teeth when thinking) and dry as paper from over-washing with Wright's Coal Tar soap – the only soap he could use without irritating his eczema. His fingers were slender from years of snap-snapping on the typewriter keys of his old Olivetti. Using only two fingers – his self-taught method – they had to move swiftly to keep up with his acuity, his glass-sharp mind. I see them now, wrapped around a tumbler of whiskey, his wireless wedged under his armpit.

Dad never wore a ring. He disliked any jewellery on men aside from wristwatches. His hands were masculine, capable, gripping the worn wood of the garden spade, which made a clean rasping sound as it sliced into soil. He would bury the bright silver edge deep (still some blood at its tip from where I'd scraped it along the granite path to carry away the corpse of a half-eaten mouse) and, slicing neatly, he would lift out a flat square of grass-fringed soil and with a squelch slap the soggy peat onto the stone.

You derived less pleasure from gardening; it seemed to make you pensive and subdued. You used to weed a lot. You had a special spongy kneeler thing and particular gardening clothes: an old pair of elastic-waisted slacks and a pink or baby-blue hairband to keep your hair off your face. Whenever we'd complain of being bored during the long summer holidays you'd ask us if we would like to help you with weeding. You would be on the far side of garden, on your knees, digging miserably, weary and melancholy. There was just too much weeding to be done in a garden too large to manage on your own and your sons kept obliterating anything new you planted with soccer balls, much to your chagrin.

In your last home, where you said you were happiest living because you didn't feel like a caretaker as you had done in our family home, you planted some new potatoes, which you grew, harvested and served up for dinner to us. You led us all outside one Sunday with pride to show them to us, sprouting up through the soil.

Now your home is inhabited by strangers. All traces of you have been sanded over, dug up, painted out. Your once cosy kitchen has been replaced by a contemporary Nordic-style minimalist one – it has featured in the property pages of some glossy magazines and has won several awards. 'Enjoy going home,' Lionel Richie's father told him once, 'because there is going to come a time when you can't go home. The house will be there but the people will be gone.' This thought is suddenly unbearable.

*

A recurring, startling horror – your body, fully clothed, tumbling, tossed, thrown, rolled, discarded with a heave high over the ground then plunging down and landing limbs jagged then battered by a violent cascade of mud and stone and rock splattering hard over your face and body, injuring it, hurting you further. 'That's nothing,' the man said as he stamped on the fledgling then shoed it out of his way.

*

No one ever held your hand, aside from that time at the party with the punch bowl, the static, instinctive shock from that intimacy forcing us both to pull our matching hands away. Not your husband, nor any of your children – even as toddlers, we hung off the crook of your arm instead or the handle of the pushchair, because your hands were always otherwise employed. Is that another reason why you were always in motion – if you were always moving, you couldn't be touched?

After Dad died you bought a new double bed to replace the two singles that had been pushed together throughout your thirty-year marriage, the gap an uncomfortable ridge that separated you. Now you could stretch out and snore with unfettered freedom. You replaced the striped brushed cotton sheets and polyester quilt with white bedlinen and an embroidered white cover. The room was fresh and airy, the sash window always slightly open. It was a gradual reclamation of space, of light and of air, a redefining of boundaries. You had made umpteen small adjustments over the years since becoming a fifty-year-old widow but you still always kept firmly to your side of the bed: nearest the door, away from the window.

The bedroom, unlike the study, was never somewhere we worried about entering for fear of disturbing our parents. All that it would expose was you at your dressing table, three views of your handsome profile in the triptych mirror, and my father in shirt and white underpants, socks pulled up his thin calves, while he got to work polishing his ancient but sedulously cared for shoes.

I don't remember ever seeing the two of you embrace, though Dad would be affectionate towards you if he had just done something to irritate or tease you, to stop things from escalating. When you set off walking, you never did so together – Dad went alone in one direction – to the office or striding along the eight miles from home to the yacht club in Dún Laoghaire every Sunday where he could read the papers in peace. 'You're the only bachelor I've ever met with five children,' a friend said to him once.

We lived on the second-most-expensive road on the Monopoly board but, unlike our neighbours, we never had any money. Its lack was the theme of all your flaming arguments. (We had to write letters to Dad, presented by you, whenever we needed new shoes.) This sense of scarcity has had two opposing intergenerational impacts – some of my siblings are extremely careful and good with money; others, like this author, are regrettably careless and impulsive.

February 1 1961
About time Feb started as I am halfway through my Feb allowance already.

*

Everyone felt, though no one said, that the occasion of your sixtieth birthday was all the more significant because you had outlived your husband and our dad, which we were extremely relieved about and grateful for. We put an almost tangible pressure on you to stay with us for as long as you possibly could. The gift we gave you of a trip to India would have been a once-in-a-lifetime holiday had your life been someone else's. The following year you made a return visit with reinforcements and wrote in your travel journal about the women you saw in Varanasi,

> *carrying enormous loads on their heads and appearing to be doing far more work than the men who were frequently asleep on the road side …*
>
> *Again the women appeared to be the beasts of burden. It is amazing how they carry such burdens, so gracefully, on their heads.*
>
> *In Pink City Hawa Mahal where the ladies of the palace observe the city while remaining invisible.*

And watching a dance *where a woman balanced an ever-increasing number of pots on her head. I think the final total was nine.*

Did you recognise your own burden in these women? Did you envy their grace and the seeming ease with which they carried their loads? Or was this the start of an awakening in you of all that you had had to endure for so long, always without complaint, never asking for help?

*

You continued many of your lifelong habits after your husband's death. The hot milk ritual and the blockbuster on your bedside table, the nightie which always made you look vulnerable and old-fashioned, belonging to a time before. You still rose early to run your bath, though even then you couldn't relax because the wretched phone would ring and you would have to gingerly step out and thump across the landing, towel not covering the important parts of you. 'Dash it! Dash it!' you would shout, in memory of your own mother, though none of us were there to hear you now that you were in the large draughty old house on your own. One day you rushed along Nassau Street and got on the 7a bus to hurry home to make Dad his lunch of pork chops before remembering, at some stage on that journey, that this was no longer one of your daily tasks.

*

31 October 1958: Didn't go to dancing class. Why? Je ne sais pas.

I have an old book of yours about ballet. It belonged to you when you were the same age as my daughter is now. Like my daughter at the same age, you dreamt of becoming a ballerina. On the inside cover you have written your name and address – Delphine Adelaide Cecilia Dudley, The Garland, Mallow, Co. Cork – in black pen with the first letter of each word traced over later in red biro. Your handwriting was upright then, no italics. When did it begin to slant? When did it all become such a rush? A desperate need to hurry through life. Did you always sense that you were running out of time?

You traced your teenage hand in pencil on the back cover of this old book – perhaps in a moment of boredom. It is inexpertly drawn, suggesting no particular artistic talent, with details of the creases around the knuckles and oblongs for the finger nails. I put my hand on top of yours. It is a perfect fit. Your fully formed hand was identical to mine. It is your hands that I can still see and remember more vividly than any other part of you, and it is in my hands that I recognise yours: they are clear and detailed replicas.

Six

Abdomen: rounded due to obesity, no alterations.

Digestive system: no lesions in the pharynx, folded oesophageal mucosa with normal appearance.

Stomach: internal folded mucosa with no lesions, gastric cavity with large amount of air and no food content.

I liked the soft feel of your stomach, covered as it always was in cotton or cashmere. You used to play with the folds of fat that accumulated below your belly button whenever you sat. You kneaded and tugged at them when they appeared like a secret exposed. You'd grab and jiggle the double fold on fold. Sometimes you would present this flesh, tray-like, your hands hammocked beneath it. Loose skin spilled over the waist of your trousers like cake mix poured into a bowl that you would then beat with vigour, and a lock of hair would come loose from where you had pinned it behind your ear, which made you all the more irritable and forced you to beat harder.

You'd tried many times to teach me the difference between stirring and folding cake batter, but I couldn't get the hang of it. You'd watch me sidelong while attending to umpteen other tasks and would finally take the bowl and spoon back from me before I'd ruined it. 'Well done, Bunty,' you would say, sounding tired, and fold the flour in the proper way and pour it out on the greaseproof paper that lined the cake tin. Then you would give me the wooden spoon and the Pyrex bowl to lick clean and while my mouth was otherwise employed you'd enjoy a few seconds of silence.

Sometimes you'd take the wooden spoon yourself and give it a swift lick at the sink, hoping you weren't being watched, but you were, always, by my myopic yet razor-focused eye. '*Mu-um*,' I would groan if you put the licked spoon back in the mixture, the way you sometimes did with baked beans heating on the hob. Food often caught in your throat in these surreptitious moments, which caused you to cough. At the theatre when you tried in earnest to suppress it, it would develop into a dry and tickly wheeze, forcing everyone sitting in our row to rock along with you as you hacked, your fingers curled in front of your mouth, just as Granny had done. These fits could be triggered by a bout of laughter or the careless ingestion of a Quality Street and would distract your family so much – with a mixture of irritation, embarrassment and concern – that our focus would be on you rather than the actors, until the interval when you could get some water and fresh air.

These coughing fits felt at times to me like an internal protest against food. Sometimes when you swallowed I imagined your epiglottis moving to block the entrance of food particles into your larynx and lungs, and your futile battle, the one I was fighting too, between want and need, between words out and food in.

You had a delicate stomach, easily upset. Your food was never adequately chewed, rather, ingested absent-mindedly while you fought a constant private battle, an inner monologue that told you to try just a small corner of the coffee cake in the fridge, closing the door swiftly, before returning moments later to cut yourself another tiny piece of icing off the top and just a small bit from the sides until all that remained was a collapse of crumbs on a circular stand and a spattering of stains down the front of your silk shirt.

I met a Frenchwoman recently who told me over lunch, as she gingerly led soup spoon to mouth, that she chose what she would wear each day based on what she was planning to eat. Tomatoes in any form were strictly out unless she was wearing a tomato shade of red.

Occasionally I would hear the thump of your feet on the landing above me in the night as you hurried from your bedroom to the bathroom to be sick. 'My stomach's a little gippy,' you would say the next morning when you couldn't face breakfast, that you were feeling 'a bit off colour', blaming it on the scallops you'd eaten at lunch the previous day. And you would look so undeniably ill, so waxy and weak, that it would make me feel a little gippy myself.

Scallops agreed with you about as much as mussels agreed with my father, though when I remember him at his happiest it's in the kitchen of our cousins' home in Connemara, in his blue linen shirt, sleeves unbuttoned and rolled to the elbow, deeply tanned and freckled forearms, grinning through his steamed-up tortoiseshell glasses, a large bowl of mussels in front of him, with their glowing mother-of-pearl insides and wet purple shells.

In my childhood, both you and Dad hated going to the doctor and rarely talked about your health; any mention of it led to talk of weight, which led to you crying with hurt and frustration. If he found you at the fridge, or tearing a ragged hunk from a packet of jelly, exhaustion and loneliness disguising themselves as hunger, he would ask, 'Do you really need that, pet?' which just made you need it more.

It was easier and more harmonious for you to leave him alone in the kitchen, where he could enjoy some revolting snack with a glass of milk, rubbing his eyes with the heels of his hands and concentrating on the harpsichord music playing on his silver tape recorder while you went to help at a sale of work for the Homeless Girls Society or to canvass for people to vote for him in the upcoming elections.

Dad would nag you about your weight, even as you ate a piece of toast with jam. He was both the cause of your gradual weight gain and the endless motivation for all of your dramatic, miserable and ultimately futile weight-loss attempts. Everyone said you looked 'smashing!' when you won Slimmer of the Year at Unislim for most pounds lost – and a prize of a sack full of potatoes, turnips and swedes.

Dad was as disciplined with food as he was with his work: porridge for breakfast every morning of his marriage and an orange that he would peel in one long curl, never stinging his perfect cuticles that displayed no gnawed-at hangnails or split skin. He kept to his daily order and routine and you facilitated this in every way. When he was a schoolboy, his father gave him every day a green apple and four squares of a quarter-pound bar of Cadbury's milk chocolate for sustenance at break time; if by chance he found himself again with the taste of apple and chocolate combined in his mouth, he was immediately four or five and could feel the Leeson Street convent school around him. In the same way, chocolate and orange for me will always remind me of my godfather and the Terry's Chocolate Orange he bought me when I burnt my finger on a cooker ring (no doubt in an attempt to reach some more food for myself).

You made kedgeree for Dad on that cooker and kippers under the grill that was so thick with old grease and charred bits of bacon that had fallen through the tray that there would often be small fires. You would quickly, calmly and with insouciance extinguish them (it had happened a hundred times before), pouring water on the flames to subdue them, yanking open the window and standing at the door, swinging the frame back and forth with vigour to create a funnel of clean air.

You mastered potato-and-leek soup early on in your marriage, but cheese soufflés were a little less predictable. We had Irish stew several nights a week, though we always left the stringy grey meat at the sides of our plates, just as we did the knobbly and unyielding kidneys from your steak-and-kidney pies.

Other foods that on seeing them or eating them bring you immediately to mind, the words alone more evocative even than their smells: cottage cheese, Ryvita, hot milk, Blue Band margarine, pink ham, picnic rolls, gooseberry fool and my favourite – ratatouille with mashed potatoes. And shepherd's pie, goulash, Ballymaloe bread, what we called Sylvanerhof – a dish of steak strips, fried onions and potatoes that we had first tasted at the Sylvanerhof Hotel in northern Italy. We stayed there only once but we remembered this dish forever. While you were cooking, you snacked on figs and prunes, and cold scraps.

Sunday, 1 July 1962: Had a rather ghastly lunch of cold scraps.

Your husband wrote you a housekeeping cheque every Monday, ignoring your tearful insistence that you couldn't possibly feed five children with that paltry amount, and you would spend it on the grocery shopping. Back you would come through the front door, humming jaggedly, fingers blanched white with the strain of plastic Quinnsworth bags filled with tins of baked beans and blocks of orange cheddar.

The stomach is like a shopping bag to hold food. A gastric cavity with *a large amount of air and no food content.* Why had you not eaten that morning? Were you feeling a little queasy? Like the time you sailed down the Ganges to the most nauseous stench of stagnant water, forging on despite having developed a sudden tummy upset in the middle of the night and woken feeling 'distinctly groggy'.

Fatty tissue is like butter, greasy and yellow, but harder to cut through. It surrounded your organs thickly, like the tatty lagging jacket on the immersion heater that was torn in places, with yellow foam exposed. Your abdomen was rounded due to obesity, no alterations – but many deep scars: vertical stretch marks. Those pale purple streaks from your belly button down were both interesting for me to examine as a child and reassuring in their familiarity.

You had all of your five babies in a nursing home, rather than a hospital, with Uncle Art delivering each of them. (A man I only knew as exceptionally elderly and who would reduce me to tears of pity as he made his shaky way to the sofa in the sitting room and lowered himself down exceedingly slowly, then fell asleep, his head lolling inches above his plate.)

When your newborn babies woke in the night you would get up to tend to them and then retire to the spare room with them so that Dad wasn't disturbed, since he had to go to work the next day.

*

'We're starving,' your daughters announced daily – a wild exaggeration that was blindingly obvious to any dinner-party guests forced to endure our gymnastics routine: two galumphing teenage girls with matching navy leotards, mottled, pale thighs and protuberant tummies. One stout, inflexible and poorly coordinated sister would thump down the hall at speed and leap on top of the even sturdier sister, stretched supine, ready to receive the weight of her sibling in her feet. Then she would straighten her legs and I would try my best to tighten my stomach muscles as she lifted me off the ground to perform aeroplane pose to halting and nervous applause.

When adolescent weight gain made this gymnastics routine a little too precarious, we employed our small brother to do the flying bit. He had a collection box for guests to contribute to in the hall – though he still insists it was a Trócaire box for genuinely starving children. This would happen before they entered the drawing room. The term comes from withdraw, a room to withdraw or retire to – though on normal days we were always immediately withdrawn from the drawing room at lightning speed. When there were guests, we had to enter it to greet them and smile as they told us how much we had grown.

'I want Fat Granny to go home,' one of your grandchildren said to you once. You pushed against the kitchen table with both hands as you stood up, the way I have to push against the steering wheel now and struggle inelegantly to get out of the car, reminding myself of you. You did go home quite quickly after that, brushing it off, smiling with your eyes closed and then turning your face away, like you did with the wooden spoon – one more thing to be swallowed and suppressed.

When our family doctor diagnosed you with low thyroid function, much later in life, you felt vindicated. 'It's an autoimmune disorder,' you said. 'I can't help it; it's not my fault.' It had a name: Hashimoto's thyroiditis. Hashimoto sounds to me like a small Japanese man on a motorbike and extremely unlikely to have anything to do with my mother or my mother's body. With this disease, your immune system attacks the thyroid – a small butterfly-shaped gland deeply embedded in the neck – which becomes damaged and can't make enough hormones. You began to take Eltroxin, a white pill like an aspirin, once a day, chalky and difficult to swallow. It helped to keep your hormone levels where they should be. But it didn't make you lose weight.

*

You avoided speaking of bodily functions as doggedly as you avoided sleep, gossip and difficult conversations.

Blood, sanitary towels, bras, body hair – all mentions were kept concealed as I stuffed stained underwear behind the white plyboard desk in my room. I learned about monthly bleeding when I stole your copy of *The Thorn Birds*. I intended to remain a tomboyish child with no aspirations to 'becoming a woman' or femininity. ('Period' was a curse word, a tease, a taunt between sisters in our home, otherwise unmentionable and shameful, I still squirm if I have to say it aloud.) When my time of the month began, I tried using Sudocrem to stop the flow. When my friend who liked to call herself the fish refused to go swimming, I confronted her with my eyes, never my words, and still she would not admit to anything having changed – though the evidence was there in the new soft, fleshy mounds beneath her *Fame* sweatshirt and the cluster of pimples on her chin. For many months I struggled with newspaper and making no sudden moves: I noticed that when I sang or sneezed or ran, it seeped through my underwear and soaked into my corduroy jeans and I was frightened that if I sat down anywhere it would be stained with dark wet streaks when I stood, so I would sit on my sleeveless blue puffa jacket instead and let it absorb the warm flow.

There was to be a trip to London to visit Buckingham Palace. I whined and nagged and threatened not to go for many months beforehand, as my shockingly poor maths sometimes confirmed that the days of bleeding would correspond to the very days of that trip, which

I was otherwise exceptionally excited about; on other days it seemed it might cease just before we set off.

You were putting clothes on the washing line – an old-fashioned rotary one held in place by a cinderblock around which the grass grew long and lush, its awkward shape making it too difficult to reach with the lawnmower, when I again said I didn't want to go to London. Why didn't you ask me why? When the thought of a trip to London would have ordinarily filled me with excitement. And when we were there, even as I was posing for photographs in my blue pakamac and navy shorts with the red piping down the sides, did you not notice that I was wedging the wads of newspaper or toilet roll back into place every time I felt the warm, heavy leak?

Why did you not leave supplies on my bed, even if talking about it was far too traumatic for us both to endure? I was pungent with puberty: sweat, blood, secretions, hot, flowing; hair, thick and long. Producing, reacting, properly vital. Though perhaps you did, when I came home – thumped my silver Chopper down the side steps, thundered up to my room to collapse into bed and rock and dream and make some sense of my overactive brain – to discover, as I approached my bed, to my utter horror, that very particular, womanly, pale-peach package, with some willowy woman in white on the front, containing thick sanitary towels like the ones that Sinead Freeney used as knee pads during hockey. Even when it was reported to you that

I was bleeding and hiding my soiled underwear behind the desk in my room, you did not confront me about it, though I would have resented you bitterly if you had dared.

I detested anything girl-related: clips, skirts, frills, pink, ribbons, bows. I resented my body for morphing into something I neither understood nor recognised. It frustrated me that I couldn't predict what was happening internally, given that it was my body attached to my head. Why was I unable to make sense of the internal workings of myself? I wondered about the actors I watched on TV – how did their minds know that their bodies were only acting? Only pretending to be terrified, bereft, miserable, dying, dead? Could playing a part that involved a lot of stress give someone high blood pressure and make them unwell? I wondered if I pretended to be more laid-back, would my body automatically become more relaxed?

I think there must have been an attempt at a conversation at some stage, but it was so excruciatingly torturous for us both – no eye contact, both our faces fixed straight ahead looking out adjacent panes of the kitchen window – that it was never attempted again. And so began many years of stealing supplies from my sister when I discovered where she had hidden them, but only when I had come to the gloomy acceptance that denial would not stop the bleeding; she, then, would be caught short and livid whenever it was her time of the month.

*

I wanted a big family – four children, certainly some boys. Motherhood to me was standing at the side of a football pitch cheering on my sons. I planned for a messy, happy, chaotic home, like the one you had given me and my siblings. I was good with children; I could do a Donald Duck impression that always made them stop crying. You said it yourself several times – and that I should consider being a primary school teacher, when all other careers looked unlikely to lead to any sort of success.

In dark moments of my infertility I wondered if I was somehow being paid back for the shame and fear and resentment I had felt at having to face puberty. Was it the endless prayers for the bleeding to stop, so I could remain forever the little boy I thought I was and wanted to be, that caused the premature ending of my cycle? The pressure I had put on my own reproductivity – to not bleed at all, please God, please make it stop! Then, years later, to please, please, please bleed – a finger inserted deep into my insides in the toilets at work when I was desperately wanting not to be pregnant, a desperate need to see blood. So many years of forcing my reproductivity to bend to my will, perhaps it was finally having its way.

After endless trying and fruitless medical interventions, I wrote in a card, *Charlie I'm pregnant*. And wrote a card soon after to tell you, too.

The first time I was admitted to hospital, I wasn't in labour; perhaps that's why my memories of it are so happy and warm. The pain and pushing was still a month away but I'd had a cold, and that morning, while waiting for the kettle to boil, I'd cracked a rib from coughing.

It was January 2009, snowing outside. The midwife on night shifts that week had been there for twenty years; she moved about the place calm and whispering, a soft pink cardigan over her white uniform. Each night she carried a tray of medicine into my cubicle: honey and lemon for my cold, peppermint water for my indigestion, and best of all, an injection of pethidine for my pain. She administered the injection to my backside, somehow never hurting me, then pulled the waffle blankets around me and told me to 'sleep tight'. And I'd float away into drug-induced ecstasy, feeling utterly safe and warm and cared for, as cocooned as the baby inside me. In the night I would hear more whispers and shuffling as expectant mothers were settled in – a bath being run, beds being made ready, the rattle of things along the corridor outside.

'I'm sure this is it, pet,' you said, forever optimistic, when I was back in the same ward a month later, rubbing your hands together in anticipation as you sat at the end of my bed. I'd been complaining of mild cramps as I ate my jelly and ice cream and watched *The Jeremy Kyle Show*. Perhaps I had a high pain threshold, I thought, maybe this labour business was really no big deal.

Twenty-four hours later I was writhing in agony, on my hands and knees on the floor, things oozing from every orifice, howling that I couldn't do it, that I'd changed my mind, that I didn't want to have a baby after all.

And then at 2.18 p.m. – such a mundane time of the day – a little animated alien appeared blinking between my legs. They had to suck her out, my poor baby, she was more distressed than her mother – it's like drowning, each time she came up for air she was pushed under again. Gargling, gurgling, water streaming out and not the right colour, but a magician in a multicoloured waistcoat appeared, tossed her about the place and made her turn pink. She was blemish-free and perfect when he handed her to me, she even came out with a side parting and her own rhythm: nibble, nibble, nibble as she took tiny tugs at my breast. New fingers, coiling and uncoiling, new eyes trying to focus on her mother's face.

*

I was back five years later, with a much more difficult pregnancy, this time without you to reassure me, staying a whole month. I became happily institutionalised, with particular things I did at particular times of the day and though I don't remember all of their names, the staff of the hospital were my daily company: the dinner lady who hid my favourite rhubarb yoghurts at the back of the fridge so there would always be one for me, the cleaner who brought in a crumpled photo of her granddaughter to show me one day. Another got me through the afternoons with talk about the son she had brought up on her own and who was top of his class at Trinity College.

Bedbound as I was, my sense of hearing seemed to become more acute and soon I could confidently recognise the different sounds: I could differentiate between the sounds of the blood-pressure monitors, the dinner trolley. The rattle of babies' cots – noisy, ancient steel transporting soft, brand-new babies swaddled in blue and pink. And even the different walks – midwives (rapid and soft-shoed), consultants (noisier, purposeful), mothers in labour (a slow trudge with occasional pauses).

On a day that I'd got some bad news about my baby, I was alone, the visitors had gone and I was thinking too much. I sat cross-legged on my bed in the dark and began sobbing, that sort of sobbing that comes from your stomach, so natural as a child but physically painful as an adult, the way an impulsive head-over-heels feels with stiff, middle-aged limbs.

A midwife I'd never met before – dark-haired, large, from the country – sat on the side of my bed. 'You'll be OK, pet,' she said, sounding like you, and rubbing her hand along my leg just as you would have done.

'You'll be OK, pet.' How those four words used to irritate me, so blasé, meaningless, offering no practical advice, an offhand way of silencing me, no sign that you were taking my circumstances seriously. But that night they comforted me like no other words possibly could, aside from the ones she said as she got up from my bed, again like the ghost of you. 'How about a nice cup of hot milk?' Not Valium, not Xanax, not two paracetamol or peppermint water, not even tea, but a nice cup of hot milk. With the comfort of her words, my cup of hot milk and waffle blankets pulled up, my tiny, worn-out little fighter and I slept soundly.

And when my second baby gave up the fight, it wasn't dramatic or violent, with sudden pains and bright blood on the bathroom floor, as had happened so many times in the seventeen weeks she'd been inside me. Each time I'd tell myself that she had gone, but each time there her tiny heart would be on the screen, beating impossibly on. When she gave up, it was a silent curling up, cutting off, shutting down. In retrospect, I feel I felt her leave; something made me lie down on the day her heart stopped beating, a sudden internal change took my energy away.

She fitted in the palm of the midwife's hand, her miniature legs dangling over its edge. I wasn't sure if I was brave enough to see her. 'Does she look like a baby?' I heard myself ask several times, and then I stopped asking that question. How unfair of me to demand that my baby look baby-like when she had done so much just to try and stay alive. The midwife laid her down on a bed of cotton wool, lifted her into a small plastic container and handed her over to me. Charlie inched forward; both of us were terrified. We looked down together at a tiny, perfect human being – everything was there and where it should have been: eyes, nostrils, lips, her lifeless arms were crossed over her minute yet somehow swollen belly. We didn't know what to do – it was torture to hold her and torture to hand her away. It was all warped, all wrong – mother and father with their newborn but their newborn was born too soon, born but dead, our baby but gone. They called her by the name we gave her: Lucia, meaning light. They encouraged us to spend time with her; they could not have been any kinder; my sister said she saw two of them cry.

That night, another midwife made me a snack of cream crackers and cheese. It must have been midnight; I was still woozy with grief and from the effects of the general anaesthetic and she had told me to stay lying down. I lay still and listened to her licking her thumb as she spread butter on each cracker, as though she were making a small meal for herself. I didn't care about that or anything else at that moment. My hunger was huge, nothing has ever tasted so good.

They hugged me – the dinner ladies, the domestics, the midwives, the consultants, the pastoral care workers – they held my hand, they sat with me for as long as they could. *C'è sempre un perché.* There is always a reason, the diminutive Italian nun told me – she had sought me out in the cafeteria when she heard our baby hadn't made it. *C'è sempre un perché.*

*

You were face up in the water when you surfaced. They said you had a peculiar expression. There was foam coming from the corner of your mouth like someone having an epileptic fit, they said, but without any convulsions. Your eyes were blinking. They thought you were drowning. The sea was incredibly strong, they said; they were afraid that you would be swept away. They found it difficult to hold on to you. (Just as I found it difficult to hold on to you.) They shouted for help to bring you ashore. They said it was difficult because you were a large lady and you were wet and slippery. A slippery fish, an eponymous dolphin, slick in your swimsuit. A robust and playful creature, at home in the sea, unwilling to leave it one last time. Your skin as smooth as a dolphin's, so you could pass cleanly through water without any drag, plunging deep under the surface and away from death.

Seven

Heart: shape and size slightly augmented, normal consistency considering the age, large vessels, aorta with a large clot in its interior.

Thoracic cavity: the pericardium appears swollen, and upon its dissection it shows a large clot that embraces the heart, the aorta shows a large haematoma and a clot in its interior.

What do you, Albert Einstein and Lucille Ball have in common? You all died from aortic aneurysms. It's called a silent killer, because there are often no symptoms until the moment one bursts. An aneurysm is a ballooning and weakening of the arterial wall and can occur in almost any artery in the body; in yours, it occurred in two places at the same time. If one grows large enough it may lead to rupture, internal bleeding, shock and death. I imagine a balloon expanding with each breath until an almighty bang, total destruction, leaving at my feet only the shrivelled remains of a once bright and joyous thing.

SUDDEN DEATH BY AN ACCIDENTAL ANEURYSM OF THE AORTA is what your post-mortem says. It's written in all caps and italics. All the As. When would an aneurysm not be accidental?

*

You were in the kitchen making dinner the night Dad collapsed. It was a Monday. He'd been cleaning out the fireplace in the sitting room. The cooker's ring was hot, ready for the searing of steaks. I wasn't there that evening – I was hoovering around tables at Pizzas & Tarts – but it was a scene so familiar that I could see it clearly and I've replayed it, in different variations, repeatedly ever since: you in the kitchen, loose strands of hair around your face, a light sheen of sweat on your forehead and upper lip, wet circles under your arms, your hum somewhat manic. Dad standing at the doorway: Aran jumper, suit trousers, slippers – black leather over grey socks. He had, seconds before, stood up from the hearth and had walked through the doorway from the sitting room. He had then put one hand on the kitchen counter closest to the door – knuckles blanching with the pressure. Did he take his glasses off, making his eyes look stark, presenting small red oblongs on either side of the bridge of his nose? He faced you at the cooker, put his hand to his chest, said nothing – and fell to the ground. In my mind he had always fallen backwards but in fact he fell forwards, onto his face. The brutal violence of the moment of impact is not easy to process.

When he fell like that (did he put his hands out to try to cushion his fall or was he already unconscious?) he slammed his bald, freckled head hard against the kitchen floor. The fall cracked the face of his Tissot watch. It was the only watch he'd ever owned, always on his wrist as his clenched fist thumped the table/door in response to your earnest requests for money for one of your children, making the cutlery jangle. If he kept his glasses on, did they fall off as he fell? Did the glass crack? Did the frame twist or break? Was he silent? Or did he cry out? What did you say as you watched him fall? At what point did you remember, in your rising panic, to remove the spitting steaks from the hot ring and turn the hob off?

My little brother ran to the family of doctors next door and in that time, while Dad lay on the kitchen floor with no heartbeat and no breath, his brain died. The doctors, when they reached him (five or seven or nine minutes later – impossible to know, because time concertinaed, lasting forever and no time at all, all at once) got his heart beating and then an ambulance turned into our driveway, he was carried into it and driven the half-mile to the hospital.

When you returned that evening, having left Dad in ICU unconscious but alive, you walked back into the kitchen and saw the two steaks, cooked, congealed. You picked up the pan and scraped them into the bin.

*

I imagined Dad's heart to be lean and taut, a muscular thing. When it clenched and ceased that winter night, none of us had expected it or prepared ourselves for it. After his death, after he fell through that doorway – through that place and space, from living to dying, and a nurse had to cut jaggedly through the wool of his porridge-coloured Aran jumper in order to reach his heart – his study, for so long impenetrable, its heavy grey metal key safe in the deep pockets of his herringbone suit trousers or beige slacks, was finally and permanently opened.

The key was lost somewhere along the line, as were those other items he had kept all his life with such care: his glasses, his fountain pen and the Tissot watch. He'd bought it in Stockholm when he was a teenager for eight or nine pounds, an expenditure then so huge he'd telegraphed home to ask for it to be authorised. I bagsed all three items after his death and lost them, of course, in a rucksack somewhere in a bedsit in Camden or maybe in Putney, my carelessness a further insult to his memory.

He valued his few possessions and kept them in good repair for many years. This is the very opposite of how I have lived but now what I admire and aspire to. To not be in constant need, always seeking to numb a hurt by filling a void, but to treasure the little you have and to polish and sew and mend and repair. His own father had a prized pair of gardening secateurs of pre-war Swedish manufacture. Many years earlier they had been missing a nut, which could not be replaced in Dublin, so Dad brought them with him on a trip to Sweden in the 1950s, with the injunction not to bother coming home if he hadn't found a replacement nut and had it fitted. He somehow managed this successfully at the local hardware shop in Lidingö, near Stockholm. This was typical of Dad: conscientious in all of his tasks.

*

A normal, healthy adult heart is about the size of a clenched fist. Dad's impatience or frustration would quicken your heartbeat and send, unseen, both his and your blood pressures soaring, thereby raising the internal temperature of the whole household. With your elbows on the table, the sleeves of your cashmere sweater pulled slightly up, tissue wedged and visible beneath the cuff, you would arrange your hands into a steeple, tapping your fingertips lightly together to dissuade tears (around now you would also close your eyes, and smile that gritted-teeth smile). Later, after an uneasy truce, Dad would get down on his hands and knees and assemble a steeple of briquettes in the grate.

You both had high blood pressure by your forties, inherited from your own parents and no doubt from their parents in turn. Dad had high cholesterol and was on medication for his blood pressure. They didn't prescribe pills for cholesterol in those days; he tried to control it through diet alone. You had high blood pressure too and something called a mitral valve regurgitation, which is quite common in older people.

You took antihypertensives and aspirin; you found them a ruddy nuisance. They gave you a cough, you frequently forgot to renew your prescription, and you were sure your heart was perfectly fine; high readings were just that white-coat thing, though your doctor insisted you wear a 24-hour monitor before you left for the Galápagos because your numbers were so high. When it tightened uncomfortably and audibly throughout your last book club meeting, everyone pretended not to hear.

*

You were the beating heart of our home. Your movements, your rhythms, your routines, always there at the centre of things, keeping everything beating. I'd lie on the bench by the kitchen table/door and whine about some injustice or nag you for something new, jiggling my foot rhythmically against the wood. Inaudible, in the event – the drumming of the needle drowned me out as you pressed your foot down on the black pedal of your Singer sewing machine. You were working on your latest Butterick pattern, the sort that came in a neat white envelope with pencil sketches of elegant women on the front. You would create something entirely different from the promising drawing, and it would probably be unwearable. Even a simpler proposition, sewing red felt double Bs (for Billie Barry Stage School) on your two daughters' white polo-neck jumpers, partially defeated you – their crookedness was immediately noticed by our Dublin city classmates, no matter how furiously we tap-danced. 'Why are your BBs sewed on wonky?' They were one more reason for us to stand out, along with our comparatively posh accents. Did we get the ferry over from England every Saturday, they asked, making us sullen for the long journey home, knowing we would never belong, you so busy reassuring us that you had to slam your foot down to avoid careening into the back of the car ahead.

*

I liked to lie against Dad's chest, listening to digestive gurgles and swirls and the gudum, gudum of his heart. We'd squash in beside him, all five of us sardine-like, at bedtime when we were at our most appealing – washed, pyjama-ed, subdued with sleepiness. He made up stories for us, about a mischievous little girl called Gloobles, who wore blue wellington boots and lived beside Mr Naughty Man and his errant son Pootle. And he would knock on my door, another beat, after his soft-slippered footfalls on the stairs and the crack of bone against bone in his knees.

In 1971, when I was two and looking for attention, you and Dad were distracted. Dad's mother had died in January that year, his father in March, and my big sister had open-heart surgery that April, at the age of just three, because 'her valve was too narrow', we were always told. She was given some stones by a nurse and had thrown fourteen of them out of the window of the room in which she was recovering. A nurse told her that it would result in the magical removal of her fourteen warts. And sure enough, when she awoke the next day, every one of them had disappeared. She proclaimed it a miracle. I reminded her of this recently, chuckling at her naivety as I retold this part of her story – but she replied that it was of course a miracle.

It was our father's heart that shut down first, it was he, not you, who whacked his head as he slammed onto the kitchen floor – again I see it, I will never not see it – his heart ceasing first, creasing himself, to use one of his phrases. The image is indelible, permanently etched in my heart and my brain. 'Ah, Bunty, that will give you high blood pressure,' he would comment about the small salt mountains I always poured at the side of my dinner plate. It would become saturated and seeping with vinegar as I waited for him to stop pestering me so I could enjoy my salty oven chips in peace.

*

On the day of your death, the tenth of February 2012, after you had been pulled from the water, after the futile attempts at CPR, when your heart had stopped beating and you had been pronounced dead, after your family had been informed of your passing, after you had been changed from your wetsuit into another, more suitable, outfit (your post-mortem states that you were *wearing clothes which are in a good state, a beige short-sleeve T-shirt with flowers of various colours, and a pair of black jersey trousers, which were properly on*) and had been put back into a Zodiac dinghy and taken by officials to a cold-storage unit on San Cristóbal Island, most of the group of women you travelled to the Galápagos with got back onto the *Legend* and continued their trip.

Only the youngest, the one who had been your snorkelling buddy and had helped to pull you from the water, accompanied your body back to Guayaquil and from there took a flight home to Dublin.

Your fellow travellers would have had to spend a few thousand euro to cancel their long-made plans and change their flights, as their travel insurance didn't cover such circumstances. I know you would have wanted them to continue with the tour, as they did.

I will never know what happened between the members of the group afterwards. There was a falling-out, but how could there not have been? When each of them was dealing with brutal shock of your leaving. None of them knew each other well. You were the one thing they had in common.

I've thought a lot about this since the day of your death, and I feel that in their position you too might have travelled on. You would have toasted the lost group member and have remembered them and cried in private and had moments of smiling, silent reflection – but you would have gone on, as far as you could and as fast as you could, from the brutal reality of the situation.

We did not criticise their actions, because even then we did as you did, not just because it is what you would have wanted but because it is in our nature having been born from you and in our nurture having been raised by you, to not criticise others' actions. But I needed to put my grief, my disbelief somewhere. I needed to attach it to something, to project my hurt and anger on someone. In the immediate aftermath their actions became a lightning rod for my grief, anger, disbelief.

I have wondered often whether things would have been different in the end if you had been a more difficult person – more outspoken, more argumentative, more demanding. If you had been a trickier woman, would it have been harder for your friends to leave you behind in the cold-storage unit on San Cristóbal? Would they still have got back on board the *Legend* if you had been a less understanding human being? Would they still have sailed away, comforting themselves in the knowledge that you would have understood? Would they have been so quick to agree that you would have wanted them to carry on with their trip, that you would, in fact, have done the very same thing? And you would have travelled on, of that I feel sure.

You have gifted me this story, your last. A story that I would not just listen to but would study forensically. After you died I was hungry for detail, parasitically pulling apart every moment – yet I cannot truly know what happened. I cannot write about it in the way that I like to, I cannot zoom in to describe in detail a series of scenes that I never witnessed or experienced.

This was a story I could have written: the dramatic event, the narrative arc, the element of shock, the dramatic plot twist. And yet, because I am from you and of you and like you and so unlike you in other ways, it was not the story I could tell, nor was it the story you would have wanted me to tell. You would have wanted me to just let it be.

Eight

Central nervous system: small haematoma in the scalp with punctiform wound that does not compromise the bone. The presence of fractures is discarded.

We each chose a mouse from your collection to put in your coffin with you. You kept this assortment of mice on the mantelpiece in your bedroom and added to it over the years. There were about two dozen of them, mostly wooden, though some were made from small periwinkle seashells, with stones for their plinths and thin pieces of twine for their tails. The smaller they were, the more you liked them.

Who gave you your first mouse? Why did you decide to begin collecting them? Did your fondness for mice begin with Disney's *Cinderella*, which featured plenty of friendly mice of that type you loved? It came out in 1950, when you were eleven. Dancing at midnight in a powder-blue dress seems to be the sort of thing you would have daydreamed about. Or did your interest in them begin with the books that you read as a child? You admired Beatrix Potter and gave your grandchildren hardback collections of her stories – perhaps your love of them began with *The Tale of Two Bad Mice*.

Mice ran freely through our house, in spite of all of my adopted stray cats. At night, silence would embolden them to explore. Along with the usual clanks and surges of the old pipes, the cistern refilling, the sporadic drip of the downstairs bathroom tap staining the base of the tub green, I could hear them scratching behind walls and skittering along the skirting boards. Or I'd startle one as I opened the kitchen door in search of a nocturnal treat and see it dart beneath the fridge, where I would sense it watching, waiting, its tiny heart galloping, its ears and whiskers twitching.

Apparently mice usually come into a home through the front door. I imagine miniature guests in top hats and calling cards, full of squeaky pleasantries and waiting for their overcoats to be taken. At times we'd be infested; more mice than humans at home, evident even during the day. We'd find them in the hot press, under the stairs, dead in a shoe, playing under our beds, between partition walls, in false ceilings, basements and lofts, behind the cooker, gnawing at the corner of the Frosties box (already compromised and cut into for tokens to send away for a bike) and once discovered by a homesick au-pair girl who, reaching into the cutlery drawer for a wooden spoon, grasped instead the brown tail of a furry visitor.

Droppings accumulated like clues under the kitchen sink, along with a close, musky odour. The stronger the smell, the nearer you were to a mouse. I would stomp down the stairs to alert them of my approach, terrified of spotting a spiky wet black ball darting from the back door. Writhing, maggoty, fluttering, clusters and infestations, the images of my recurrent nightmares.

A memory: the boyfriend who told me about a rat who nursed on a sleeping woman's breast in Holles Street hospital. This same unreliable boyfriend described you as 'bumptious', a word I had never heard before. I looked it up – it means irritatingly self-assertive, everything you weren't and he was. He told me to look it up to use in one of my stories.

Dad loved that you weren't bothered by mice, that you didn't stand screaming on a chair like those women he considered silly and vacuous who became hysterical at the sight of a tiny defenceless animal. You would greet them casually and chat to them affectionately if you happened to spot one while you worked on your sewing machine, your nail-less toe in Scholl sandals pressing the black shining pedal.

You never harmed a mouse or did anything about ridding the house of them. Not so your errant former son-in-law, the farmer, who once threw a cup of scalding water over a baby mouse in the corner. He would poison them too, reducing the ability of their blood to clot so that they bled internally and died slowly, or set a trap with a spring-loaded bar that swung down rapidly and with force, breaking the mouse's neck or spinal cord, crushing its ribs and skull.

The presence of fractures is discarded. Despite the trauma of your death, it was a source of profound comfort to find that your body, when it came back to us, was unbroken, still complete externally. You were/are dead but you didn't break anything when you died. The final transformation had surged through you internally, but externally you were just as you had been when you entered the water, preserved and then embalmed in your entirety. You were not outwardly injured or disfigured in any way, aside from the small cut on your forehead. The embalmers couldn't have known that you never looked angry when they worked on preserving your face.

*

After I had lost you, lost Lucia, was losing Charlie (though I don't like the term lost, as if I were somehow careless in mislaying you and should have taken better care; it was I who was lost when all three of you had gone), I met a woman who claimed to be a psychic. The unscrupulous ones can spot the lost, the vulnerable, the grieving.

This one claimed that she could communicate with you. She conned me into parting with a huge amount of money. (I'm too ashamed to tell you how much.) It was money you had left me and the way she did it was by the entirely coincidental presence of a small wooden mouse on the edge of the table where she did her first reading for me. Though she called you my ma and attributed to you words and sentences that you would never have uttered, which made her sound like an entirely unrecognisable person, it was the sight of this small mouse on her desk that was sufficient to convince me. In a world that made no sense, here, finally, was a concrete sign. When I mentioned the mouse, she gave a knowing smile.

We all grasped at signs, as the grieving do: robins, double rainbows, lightbulbs blowing, feathers, butterflies, dragonflies. The song you loved written by your eldest son, the musician, that was playing in a café on the day we visited the undertakers to choose your coffin. Unexplainable coincidences – we took them for evidence that you were still in the ether around us, still somehow present. We needed to regain some sort of control of our lives, and so we clung on to these portents from beyond. I was in an endless subconscious conversation with you, so that when someone mentioned you in real life, I felt that was a strange coincidence too. I was just talking to her, I'd want to say.

Why did you pause on the doorstep to wave goodbye to me that evening? When it was not in your nature to ever pause, especially with so much still to get ready for your trip? Ordinarily, you would have shut the heavy front door straight away (though we would hear your voice continuing to converse with us on the far side of it – not the words, but the sound) while we were walking away down the path, and have immediately busied yourself with pressing things. Why did I tell myself to remember seeing you there – or was it only after you were gone that the memory implanted itself? Why did you run back upstairs at the very last moment to get a small toy for your granddaughter? A Beanie Boo Dalmatian dog that she called Delphine and took, along with her sucky blanket, everywhere for many years after.

Why is the robin on the branch of that tree not moving? Why is it staying perfectly still even as I move closer? And it's a cherry tree, like the one we had in our garden and which has ever since reminded me of you, along with countless other things (mice of course, but birds too and dolphins, because of your name and your love of the sea). Just as I reach for my phone to capture this moment, heavy with symbolism, it flies away. And then a bird slams into the car windscreen on the journey home – a violent smack, like something thrown in anger, like a suddenly-flung black rock. I wonder how to find comfort from this surely ominous sign. The internet says that to see a bird hitting a window is a sign of money worries. (How does the bird know I am worried about money?) Birds are also sometimes seen as portents of doom and death.

When we were emptying your kitchen, my sister opened the cupboard where the saucepans were kept and found, on top of a saucepan lid, a tiny crystal mouse. How could anyone possibly explain that? We took it as a sign, because we needed to, signs were what we had left.

*

Charlie shared your fascination with mice; he and his brother used to breed white mice at their home in Bangor and sell them to the boys at their grammar school. You and he were closer in age than he and I were, but you accepted him without question and guessed at our attachment before I ever mentioned it; I pointed to his photograph in *IMAGE* magazine and you knew, seeming to sense instinctively that this separated man in his fifties with an iguana was already significant to me.

And he liked you immediately. You bought his paintings for your family, for yourself and for your friends, and you loved to talk to him about art. You had studied for a degree in art history and volunteered at the National Gallery of Ireland, and Charlie always had the sense that you wanted to impress him with your knowledge of his profession – which was a little unfair but probably true.

The rhythm and dynamic of my relationship with Charlie was a sort of replaying of your dynamic with Dad. I would do my best to keep him happy and calm, watching him sidelong whenever we were in company, just as you always watched Dad, to try to gauge his mood, to make sure that he was comfortable, that all his needs were being met.

You were the sort of person who said sorry when someone else stepped on your foot. I hear your apologies in mine when something goes wrong, irrespective of fault, whether I was even there or not. I take the blame, assume responsibility, it was always my fault. The way I was with Charlie, it was a learned behaviour. As soon as Dad arrived home, we would scatter like woodlice exposed by an upturned rock while you would move towards him to help him, to ease his burdens, to serve him.

Charlie edited the first draft of my debut novel. He said I used the word Mum far too much in my writing – which I did and still do. His illness developed just around the same time as your death, his slow decline in the vastly narrowed world of a nursing home in dramatic contrast to your suddenly being submerged under the warm, exotic waters of the eastern Pacific Ocean.

As I became less dependent on him, he became more reliant on me. We didn't know it then but something was going very wrong with his central nervous system.

A friend is surprised that I can't bear the thought of never talking to Charlie again. She doesn't understand why I don't feel this about losing you, my mum. It's because I am always in conversation with you. But as I write these words now I realise that they are not quite accurate. It's not that I am always in an active conversation with you aloud, or even within my own thoughts, and it's not so much that I feel your presence around me in any sort of material or ethereal way – it's more that you are always, always in my thoughts – my waking thoughts and my dreams. It's constant, not a yearning or even nostalgia, it's just that I see you in me; in everything I do and everything I do badly that you would have done well. It's constant and permanent and perhaps why I've found finishing this book so very hard. But you will still be there in the way I use my hands, in how I see myself in repose, in my siblings and even in my child, in my body as it ages and in old photos of youthful you, at the backs of drawers or hung prominently on walls.

*

In the seventeenth week, the baby develops hearing. It can hear its mother's voice. Did my baby Lucia hear my voice, my saying as we drove back from Rosslare that I felt suddenly, desperately low? As I were cutting off the blood supply between us and she was curling up and dying? Did she hear my voice for the first time as she was dying? Did Dad hear my voice for the last time as he was dying? Did he hear me externally? Did my baby hear me call for her from within? Or was one too early, one too late? Both a silent severing of ties?

Nine

Head well placed, grey hair dyed blonde, with large amounts of sand in its full extension.

It's impossible for me to imagine you with any hairstyle other than your girlish bob. It's a myth that a person's hair continues to grow after death. A hair's follicle needs oxygen to provide it with the energy to grow. Once the heart stops pumping oxygen around the body in the blood, the energy supply dries up, and so does the cell division that drives hair growth. Your hair did not grow after you died, any more than you ever let it grow in your lifetime. It was your defining feature, platinum blonde, making it easy for us to spot you in a crowd. We were always, always searching for you, from the moment you left our sides.

There's a photograph I have seen only once and have searched for periodically since, without success. There are two girls in the foreground, perhaps in their late teens, their arms linked at the elbows. They are caught in a moment, captured as they are walking, talking, both looking away from the camera so that their faces are in profile. For those one or two seconds, they stand very still. The coats they wear tell us that it is winter; the light suggests early evening. Behind them, shop windows are lit up in the dusk; it is a city street.

The girl on the left is you. You are standing beside your friend Valerie Danby-Smith, whose short, curly black hair was the sort you said you always wanted for yourself; your own hair is dark blonde, softly waved, shoulder length, deeply parted and tucked behind one ear in the style of Marlene Dietrich or Grace Kelly, and held in place with Elnett.

Your smile is soft, your averted eyes gentle and warm, your expression dreamy, faraway. You look as though you are aware, albeit modestly, of your beauty: the slight upward tilt of your chin, the lightness of your gaze. You are wearing a long, grey herringbone coat that reaches your slim shins. Your shoes are dark-brown or black lace-up brogues. You still have eyebrows – neat and dark. Your nose is perfectly straight, your skin, cold-cream smooth and taut around your fine features.

Were you more yourself in this photograph, before we ever knew you? When you were inchoate, primitive? You look like someone very different from the wife, mother, chatelaine who gave and gave and gave and built a sturdy wall of insulation around herself, protective, numbing cladding, a cocoon. Is this the truest version of you? Is the girl in the photo the Delphine that none of us, your children, ever met?

Who is behind the camera? What is the occasion? What shop window are you facing? Is it Switzers, or Greene's bookshop, or are you on O'Connell Street outside Clerys or Henry Street at Arnotts? Perhaps you are on your way to an evening event at Trinity College?

Small shards of you in silver and white, fleeting glimpses of the girl you were, dashing about town, trying and failing to study, painting the flat, meeting your father for lunch at Jammet's, worrying about money, frustrated with yourself, self-effacing and gently self-mocking. Harried, innocent. Sweet-natured. Immersed in the memory of the photograph, I find myself entering the intimacy of your life then and missing someone I never met, a version of you before all of us. You in a tweed winter coat, racing to lectures in the stinging sleet – I see you always in foggy, wintry, silvery grey light and hear the voice of the girl you were, summoning it to my ear, bell clear. Here I am reading about you before I ever met you and writing about you after you knew me.

You took the Trinity entrance exam and got into the School of Law, one of only a few women who did so. You worked for a law firm called Potterton's (the name suggesting to me kettles and cosy things) when we were young. Later, when we were less dependent on you, all in secondary school, you got a diploma in library and information studies at UCD and established the library in the law firm of A&L Goodbody.

6 January 1958: Horrible day and I was rather depressed at leaving but I am returning on Friday, DV. Had a rather complicated journey home and for some unknown reason bought myself a pink hat.

11 January 1958: I was packing most of afternoon – don't believe in travelling light.

17 January 1958: Read through Bacon's essays – like wading through thick, sticky mud.

24 January 1958: Rushed around town slaughtering time.

7 February 1958: More snow, painting at a stop as financial embarrassment however managed to borrow some money from office and more or less finished it.

8 March 1958: Another castle in the air has crashed to the ground but there is so little I can do about it.

21 January 1959: Indian dining lecture very interesting. Made me want to see India more than ever.

21 June 1959: Went to tennis party at Veronica's house, enjoyed it thoroughly except when I had to play tennis.

1 October 1959: Shorthand and typing class rather conducive to sleep.

27 November 1959: Got hair set and brightened quite effectively in the morning.

11 December 1959: Rather difficult to say when the day started as I didn't go to bed.

After Dad died, you did a degree in history of art followed by one in archaeology. You volunteered in the Chester Beatty museum, the National Gallery of Ireland and, for as long as I can remember, the

Homeless Girls Society (the stickers of which I coveted as a child) and the Dublin Boy Singers. I found a flier for a bring-and-buy sale amongst your boxes recently. *Please support Delphine* you had scribbled under the details, adding no comma.

The photograph that I still remember so well was black and white and had a thin white border, as photographs did then, and the circular indented watermark of the photographer or his studio; a raised seal produced by something called the dandy roll process. I found the watermark pleasingly tactile; I traced my fingers around its ridges.

There was no inscription on the back, where it was grubby from various fingers that handled it and handed it on to others at other mealtimes over the years, finally to lay it face down and perhaps rest a wine glass or a coffee cup on it, leaving behind tiny bits of dissolved, unidentifiable dirt.

And the two young women? Valerie became Ernest Hemingway's secretary; she travelled with him to Paris to revisit scenes of his youth – the Paris of Joyce and Fitzgerald – before he became depressed, underwent shock treatment and ultimately committed suicide, nineteen days before his sixty-second birthday. In 1967 Valerie became a Hemingway herself when she married Ernest's son Gregory, later Gloria. You married an up-and-coming academic and became a politician's wife, mother of five, a law librarian and holder of more than one degree. You kept in touch – Valerie later wrote a book about her life with the Hemingways and came to visit you in your home in Dublin.

*

Whenever you swam, your preternaturally blonde bobbed hair would be tucked into a tight latex swimming cap. You hated getting your hair wet, hated washing it. When you swam, you would never put your face under the water. Instead, you held your head high, your neck looking uncomfortably strained.

Large amounts of sand in its full extension – but then, how did your hair become so full of sand? Did the force of the wave drag the swimming cap off your head? Perhaps it was when your body was back on the beach and people were pummelling you, attempting CPR, to bring you back to us.

The sand would have annoyed you – I can hear the scratchy scrunch, can even feel the particles under your nails as you scratch your scalp, had you been able to feel it. A billion tiny specks of what could become glass invading every part of your face – nose, hair, ears.

It was February the tenth, just noon in Gardner Bay and already darkening in Dublin, with the six-hour time difference between Ecuador and Ireland. I was lifting my child, not quite three years old, onto the monkey bars in the back garden.

In Irish time, you were still alive. Under the water it is still not true, before the calls are made from a different time zone, until the phone is answered. You are still on holidays, still having a wonderful adventure, still with us, still fine. My mother is wonderfully healthy and well. Until one of your group, the oldest friend, back on board the boat in Gardner Bay, phoned her husband on her mobile, at home, who told Uncle James who told Aunt Rowena who told my sister. She was in Life Style Sports with a friend, aimless, chatting, when she received the call.

Physically cautious always, I would have been holding my daughter constantly on the bars, never would have let go, never allowed her arms to stretch and dangle unsupported, her little plump legs flailing. The fearless toddler boy beside her was ruddy-cheeked and in his element. His mother and I were still in that halting, getting-to-know-each-other phase. She was the friend the psychic said my mother had chosen (although they had never met) as a vessel through which to communicate with me.

When it was completely dark, we cajoled our toddlers indoors. And this I remember – a feeling of well-being: the cold wet air, the smell of the turf fire Charlie was lighting upstairs, the honey-coloured lamplight of the kitchen. Charlie called me from the top of the stairs. His voice sounded strange: dark and formal. He told me to please come up to the sitting room. I followed him up with mounting dread – I thought the kids must have damaged one of his possessions. He led me into the sitting room and encouraged me onto the sofa.

I didn't understand why he wasn't balancing on the edge of the coffee table as he liked to do – forever a boy, predictably unpredictable.

My sister had phoned him. She couldn't face calling me directly to tell me such crushing news. Charlie told me that you had been swimming, that there was a big wave, that you had died, were dead. I couldn't move for several minutes and then I couldn't stay still, not for days, months, years, not even now.

*

Much later we would hear the details from my brother and his wife, who travelled to Ecuador to bring your body home. The undertaker with long, pointed fingernails who had greasy hair that was pulled back with steel wire. The guards armed with machine guns at the hotel in Guayaquil (the largest city in Ecuador, and one that suffers from significant crime), the power outages that regularly left their floor in complete darkness. The black, coffin-shaped cover over your coffin at Amsterdam, the sight of which caused dozens of travellers to fall silent.

It was your son who left his home in Boston to bring you back to us all. The tenth of February is his wife's birthday. He wouldn't have ordinarily been travelling for work – he tried to put special dates aside on his calendar – but there was a conference in Florida his boss had asked him to speak at. The boss writes the cheques, so my brother agreed and promised his wife he would be back by that evening so they could celebrate the rest of her birthday together.

In Florida, speech made, he was in a taxi heading back to the airport when he turned on his phone to hear a message from my sister – his sister; your eldest daughter – sounding serious and distressed and asking that he call her back immediately. He guessed from the tone of her voice that something had happened to you. She told him the story briefly: you had gone swimming, a big wave had hit you, you had been found floating face up in the water.

The relative times are confusing. The time difference between Ireland and Boston is five hours for most of the year, but in February Boston and Ecuador are in the same time zone. Perhaps there was a delay in making the phone call – entirely understandable in the summoning up of courage to contact us, her family. There was no time, only panic.

Someone had to identify your body. My brother phoned his wife with the news as he queued at security at Miami International Airport, about to fly back up to Boston. The next day they flew together from Boston back to Miami and from there on to Guayaquil. They met the Irish consul for Ecuador at the hotel.

It was late in the evening when they arrived and they found Guayaquil a sinister, frightening place. Located close to the equator, it has the same temperature as Singapore – thirty-two degrees and humid, all the time. They couldn't leave their hotel. They tried once and somebody tapped his wife on her shoulder and told her to put her phone back in her purse and get back to wherever they had come from. Apparently a number of tourists had been kidnapped off the streets, thrown into cars.

So they retreated to a Bavarian restaurant inside the hotel. The restaurant wasn't particularly good and they thought it was interesting that a hotel in Ecuador wouldn't have a restaurant that represented anything about Ecuadorian cuisine. Perhaps most of its guests were Ecuadorian. Given the kidnapping danger, it didn't seem to be a popular tourist destination.

The Irish honorary consul to Ecuador arrived the following day; as it was such a dangerous city, she kindly stayed with them the whole time. Your son organised a car service to take them to the mortuary first, to identify you.

Your son did not want to see you in death. He was disturbed by the thought that you wouldn't have been wearing a very stylish bathing suit. (That my brother would have any notion of the current fashion in swimsuits if it walked up and grabbed him was jolting and at the same time moving.) The memory that he wanted to stay with him was of running towards you in the garden in the sunshine as a small child and you with your arms held out to catch him.

He remembers the four of them – him, his wife, the consul, the person who worked there, standing in a white, antiseptic-smelling room for a very long time.

There was a big metal table to one side and a small bank of drawers on the right. The employee opened one of the drawers and then he said something to the consul, and your son and his wife were taken aside.

They only opened the drawer halfway. You were wrapped in gauze, or whatever it was they used to transport you in. Perhaps your body had deteriorated and they thought it would be too upsetting. The consul told them it wasn't usually like this, but that since they had her passport and driver's licence, she would go back by herself and identify you that afternoon.

Your son then had to go to a public records office in Guayaquil to get your death certificate. The building was large and busy, filled with people registering births and deaths. At the front of the queue, the consul acted as interpreter. The city employee was initially very matter-of-fact, but at some point in their conversation it seemed to have struck him that this was a man's mother and he became a lot more empathetic as he recognised the sorrow of the situation.

At the mortuary, an elderly woman led your daughter-in-law to a room where all your belongings had been thrown on a bed. She had to sort through your suitcase to find clothes you could be dressed in for your journey home. Everything was jumbled up, she said, it was a mess. The elderly woman stood in the corner, entirely silent, until everything was packed.

Back at their hotel that evening, power outages began. Everything went black. Dislocated voices floated through the profound darkness of the hallways. They called the front desk repeatedly to try to tell them about the blackout on their floor. The staff didn't understand anything they said. They later found out that power outages were frequent because there wasn't enough electricity.

The phone rang constantly. There was a lot of paperwork involved with getting your body out of the country. There was nothing my brother and his wife could do but sit there and wait. For several days they went to the gym and used the treadmill, then sat in a little courtyard in the middle of the hotel and tried to figure out the route they would take to bring you home to Dublin.

They had to wait for your body to be embalmed before they, and you, could leave Ecuador. The most important thing was to ensure that you got back to Dublin safely; they had to be certain you were with them for the entirety of the long trip home. At the airport, the security guards went through every piece of luggage, gesticulated at the owner of belongings that had set off the alarm, ordered them to collect their luggage and to go back through the security gates again.

They, you, the three of you, took a fourteen-hour flight from Guayaquil to Amsterdam. In Amsterdam, everybody was milling around at the departure gate waiting for the flight onwards to Dublin. In a single moment the airport seemed to become entirely silent as the crowd who were standing near the window watched as your body was being carried into the hold of the plane in a large black case that contained your coffin. Your son had to look away. Everyone was quiet, reverent.

The five of us met at Dublin Airport arrivals, each of your children but almost unrecognisable. Each of us stunned, fragile, incapable of judgement or aggression or resentment, in a hollowed-out huddle, hugging and smiling your rueful smile. The feeling of overwhelming exhaustion. The fatigue of grief is staggering.

After

THE LAST THING YOU DID ON THE LAST DAY OF your life, before lowering yourself into the water of Gardner Bay, was to pose for a photograph on the beach. You are wearing a black T-shirt over a black swimsuit, standing with your feet already at the water's edge. Your body is facing towards the sea but you are looking back, over your shoulder in the direction of the shore. Did someone call your name to make you turn around? Shout at you to say cheese? Even then, you are not looking directly into the lens, but somewhere just beyond. Could anyone see by your hazy, detached eyes that the process of your leaving had already begun?

*

'Now, have you got everything?' you always asked as I was leaving you, pulling my head distractedly towards your chest and kissing me dryly on my hair. 'Did you get much done?' I know you would me ask now, with such a tone of dismay in your voice, of disappointed resignation, that you won't wait for my reply.

This book has been the hardest to write. It's the shortest of all my books but it's taken so very long to finish. I have come up against the deepest resistance to ending it, to letting it go. Our long chat will have to come to a close and I will feel another end. Having put you back together again, I will have to finally let you go.

When I first read the report of your death in notes translated from Spanish and sent to the family by the honorary consul to Ecuador a year after your funeral, I had a strong and urgent sense that I could still alter the outcome. That I could write it differently, with a different narrative arc and an alternative ending, one in which you got a terrible fright and gave yourself an almighty bang on the head but later told us how you had been looked after so wonderfully by the hospital staff though the thought of eating the following day, as you sat up in your hospital bed, did make you feel a little queasy.

I could make the ending more prosaic. It was a horrible accident but thank God you are absolutely fine, just thoroughly bored confined to bed. You simply lost your footing, you would tell your friends, your family, over Sunday lunch back in Dublin.

Or maybe you recovered so quickly that there was no need for hospital at all. 'I'll be totally fine,' you'd say to your panicking friends and alarmed bystanders. Then, keen to divert attention, 'Look at those funny fellows,' you'd add, pointing towards the seals, to allow you a few seconds to regain your composure.

We printed too many memorial cards. To bin or recycle the surplus felt irreverent, wrong. And so they have been passed around the family, in a collapsing cardboard box, from my sister's spare room to my brother's attic and now to mine, where they sit on the floor to the side of my writing desk, which used to be yours, with a miscellaneous assortment of other things I no longer need but can't yet part with. At the bottom of one of your own boxes of miscellaneous things, I find your parents' extra memorial cards – you also printed too many. It's a difficult number to predict – how many to expect at a funeral.

At the undertaker's in Dublin I felt a profound need to see your body, to know for certain that it was you. Your second son, on the other hand, still didn't want to see you lest it would interfere with his remembering you in life. When I looked into the coffin there was a moment of alarming relief: 'That's not Mum!' I said aloud, when I saw the angry, purple, thickly-caked skin of the corpse. Someone put their hand on my shoulder and encouraged me away.

I don't know who translated your post-mortem from Spanish before the consul sent it on to us. Some of my siblings didn't want to read it, but I had to look close, as close as I possibly could, to see into every dark corner.

And as I read the description of your body in cold, scientific terms, its flaws and details so familiar to me, so profoundly comforting, so beautiful in their imperfections, I felt the need to piece you together again, to put flesh back on bone, to bring you back to life in words, one by one. To try to see you clearly now that you were finally still. To take you out of the steam-filled kitchen, to remove your apron and your slippers, to put you centre stage.

The beginning of this book seems very far away. At the start there was the problem of tenses – as there often is in the immediate aftermath of a death. Mum is/Mum was, Mum does/Mum did – the swift correction, the awkwardness, the jolt of realisation. When did we start referring to you in the past tense? Present continuous, past, present. Simple present, present perfect, present perfect continuous. You are still in the present; for a long time none of us could talk about you in the past.

I could only write this book to you, in the second person. *Generally, it is best to avoid second-person pronouns in writing because they remove the distance between the reader and the writer*, a quick internet search instructs me.

In the hours after you died, along with the brutal shock, I remember feeling two unexpected emotions: lightness and relief. Nothing mattered any longer now that you were dead. The very worst thing had happened and life was now cancelled. I didn't have to work, or to meet people or to pay bills. And I no longer had to worry about keeping you safe. I had feared your death and had prayed to keep you alive for so many years, ever since Dad had died – and now you were gone, and everything was permanently and radically altered. The permanent dread of your death was not something I needed to worry about any longer. I felt that I was free-falling.

'At least you were with them when they died.' 'They would have sensed your love.' 'Hearing is the last thing to go.' 'How special that you were all there, that you got to say goodbye.' I said these phrases so many times, utterly confident in my assumption (the blasé certainty of a person not yet acquainted with grief) that I knew what I was talking about and that the words themselves would offer some sort of balm – and also with a bleak sort of competitiveness and resentment. Others had what I missed out on with both of my parents, having had no time to prepare for that moment (despite forever predicting and imagining and dreading it). Both of their collapses were as catastrophic as a high-speed collision.

*

The three Dublin-based siblings met at my sister's home the evening after the phone call and I felt another unexpected emotion – the strong and comforting sense of connection and support that comes when people who care about each other and who are going through a similar experience gather. It felt oddly cosy – like being snowed in together, or stuck in a lift, or communally plunged into the darkness of a power cut, each of us fumbling to find our way. We busied ourselves with things to be done, just as you would have.

Two days later, the most powerful wave of grief came over me while I was in the bathroom, brushing my teeth. I simply could not tolerate the pain of your loss. I just could not stand it in that moment; I couldn't carry on – in a wild panic, a sudden realisation that all was lost, I lowered myself onto the closed toilet seat and gave up telling myself I had to be brave. My sister felt floored by a sudden wave of it too – she was halfway down the stairs at home when her grief became so overwhelming that she sank to her knees on the landing, entirely unable to move. I remember the same sense of bleakness and despair in the days after Charlie was diagnosed. I just couldn't and wouldn't tolerate losing him. And I remember crying so persistently on a solitary drive to Glasnevin Cemetery to visit my baby Lucia's plot that I couldn't see the road ahead.

In those early days, weeks and months after losses, I felt a profound resentment of anyone whose family was intact and functioning, and fiercely, ferociously protective of my daughter. I was furious that she was being denied a happy, straightforward childhood, the sort it seemed all my friends' kids had. I felt that events had somehow damaged her irreparably. Yet for all she has lost – father, grandmother, sister – she has gained precious and invaluable gifts: resilience, empathy and a maturity far beyond her years.

I am an entirely different mother to my child than you were to me. I explain everything, everything. I overshare. I couldn't put her down as a baby, couldn't stand to hear her cry. I tell her I love her at the end of most conversations; I give her names for different moods. She is a feisty, hilarious, outrageous, pugnacious, formidable, remarkable character.

C'è sempre un perché. I finally understand, all these years later, what these words mean. The words spoken by the small Italian nun after Lucia had died. There is always a reason, and the reason I see now is that I could never have managed – emotionally, logistically – to have parented any more than the one child I have, or to have had enough love or patience in reserve.

*

Whenever I describe my various losses to others – recounting facts I've told so often that I've stripped them of emotion and become immune to their impact – I see shock on their faces, their heads tilt with pity. I think my detached delivery is probably at least partly a self-protecting mechanism to cushion me against the shock, the sadness and the trauma – and to convince myself that I am bulletproof now.

When you died, when Charlie was diagnosed, when we lost Lucia, I thought it would be impossible to be happy again, that I would always be grieving for you and for them. And though I always will be grieving – and this has been another surprising thing about grief for me – rather than despairing or becoming consumed in misery, as time passed I felt, and still feel, spurred on by those missing people whom I have loved so deeply and a determination, more than ever, to strive to do all I can, not just to make the best of things, not just to muddle through, but to really thrive.

For me, when the initial numbness of grief subsides, everything takes on more significance. There are still some negative emotions at times – rage, hurt, confusion, sadness – but I feel that life has become much more meaningful, more multi-layered and somehow more beautiful now that I have experienced grief. Such darkness makes any brightness seem all the more vivid and profound.

Grief gives life more meaning. There are still days of numb greyness, nothingness and others where everything feels heightened, when the smallest thing can reduce me to tears, when I am so filled with emotion and with no place to put it, to express it, needing to sing, needing to cry, feeling everything too acutely.

*

And now I have done what I can to pull you out of the mortuary, to let you rest whole and at peace. I have brought you back to life so that I can say goodbye to you, shine a light on you, and live on like you. As my body ages, it becomes more like yours and we are not further away but closer now than we have ever been.

I have set out to make you fully animated again so that I can finally leave you. I wanted to move in more closely, as if viewing a painting at a gallery, before moving away and walking on and leaving the subject of the painting behind. But grief is never complete and I will never not be in conversation with you. I will always need to see you in every mouse, in that particular shade of powder blue, in every serendipitous event or seeming coincidence.

To finish this book is another leave-taking. I wanted to linger in this liminal space, not get over, not get through it, not move on. But our conversation has not ended, it is infinite. Whenever your name is mentioned, less often as you fade in others' memories, I think and sometimes say, 'That's strange, because she and I were just chatting.' Ours are blurry, half-conscious conversations – I can't hear your voice and I don't speak audibly in reply, but it's a steady, ongoing, silent internal conversation, an awareness, between the two of us.

It is you that I'm talking to and with, but a version of you that is somehow inside me and at the same time beside me, devoid of colour, never with the yellow-gold that always surrounded you: sun, sunny, light, yellow, yellow car, yellow dress, yellow hair, yellow cheese soufflé bubbling, yellow T-shirt with a yellowy olive-oil stain down the front.

*

I can never find your grave, despite the parsley, sage and rosemary that was planted in the fertile ground of the graveyard and is now so abundant. Your eldest son planted these bushes with the idea that visitors to the grave could take some sprigs home, but there are fewer visitors as time goes on and memories fade. One day, you will be little more than a clickable image on an online family tree – just a name, some dates, perhaps an adjective or two.

One day I too will be summed up in a few adjectives, or with an oft-repeated story. Reduced to a character trait, a funny or tragic anecdote. In conversation around a dinner table, we will all be little more than a memory, a first name, eventually faceless, characterless, until we disappear into a distant, entirely forgotten generation.

*

At first, my siblings and I all grieved differently – either wanting no detail or all the detail. 'Eat a steak,' someone said. 'You look destroyed,' said another. 'You will be on your knees with grief for years,' they said, but they didn't understand. We'd lost another layer of skin, the protective layer. We were exposed, so tired.

Then we did as our mother did, we turned something tragic from being awful into the most beautiful, idyllic death. It's in our genetics. We five siblings used to stamp on each others' heads and give each other knuckle punches and Chinese burns, but now that we are orphans we couldn't be any closer.

We turned it into a beautiful end – because we are of you and made from you and ultimately we are turning into you and following in your swift footsteps. We reworked the narrative. We talked about dolphins. We gave you a happy ending. Dying exactly as you lived, you died when you were still vital, and still vital to us, still surrounded by love, plunging joyfully into the great unknown. We turned your death into an absolutely fitting end to a mother with a lifelong hatred of hospitals and with a profound love of sea swimming.

This is the narrative we settled on, and the story became fact because we come from you and will always contain so much of you.

*

You would have been furious not to have been at the funeral. To see such a turnout, so many in the church that there was standing room only at the back. One of your grandchildren brought up a mouse from your collection at the offering of the gifts. Another brought up a book of yours called *1,000 Places to See Before You Die*, bookmarked at Machu Picchu, which you hadn't yet got around to. There were also a Scrabble board and a pair of ballet shoes.

You had unintentionally given us a lot of time to prepare for your funeral, because it took nine days to bring you home. There was gentle competition between us, an unspoken pressure to make the most perfect choices for the ceremony – what readings would you have liked? What piece of music would represent you best? What photo and font should we use for the leaflet? Impractical suggestions were not shouted down or criticised but greeted with cooperative decisions, coming together as siblings, doing this last thing. The ingrained traditions of the Catholic church provided profound comfort, even while some or all of us no longer went to Mass on a regular basis or were even, at this point in our adult lives, confirmed atheists. They were things we knew from our childhood, like you.

We chose a reading from the Book of Wisdom (3:1–9). 'In the eyes of the unwise, they did appear to die, their going looked like a disaster, their leaving us like annihilation.'

The priest told me that the piece I chose for your recessional, 'In Paradisum' from Fauré's *Requiem*, was the most beautiful piece of music ever written. I had a feeling of pride that I had won the silent contest with my siblings, still and forever vying for parental approval.

Father C read a poem – this he chose himself, confident in the knowledge that it was just the right thing: you had given him the perfect twin themes of the sea and death. He himself died less than six months later.

'Gone From My Sight' by Henry van Dyke

I am standing upon the seashore. A ship, at my side, spreads her white sails to the moving breeze and starts for the blue ocean. She is an object of beauty and strength.

I stand and watch her until, at length, she hangs like a speck of white cloud just where the sea and sky come to mingle with each other.

Then, someone at my side says, 'There, she is gone.'

Gone where?

Gone from my sight. That is all. She is just as large in mast, hull and spar as she was when she left my side.

And, she is just as able to bear her load of living freight to her destined port.

Her diminished size is in me – not in her.

And, just at the moment when someone says, 'There, she is gone,' there are other eyes watching her coming, and other voices ready to take up the glad shout, 'Here she comes!'

And that is dying …

Here she comes, but it is not you at seventy-two. Or even you at fifty. Or you at twenty, impossibly beautiful. You before I ever knew you and yet how I will always remember you. The version of you that I remember most clearly is the version that was you at your most yourself, long before I was born.

You have set your book down because your daddy is calling you. You run down the laneway of Lugdine Park, the holiday home in Glengarriff. Your dog, Bobby, is by your side, your blonde bobbed hair is held back in a clip, your ankle socks white, you run as fast as you can to the postbox – but you don't stop there, you giggle at your boldness as you run on, your father fading in the distance. In my mind, you leap and plunge into the inky, still sea – but you are fully dressed, so how could this be? And yet I see you swim out towards Garnish Island and out of view.

I see you above the glassy surface of the water, waist-high, picking your way outwards, navigating rocks in slippery flippers, giant-stepping. And again I see your body, carried by undulating waves; surging forward, then being sucked back by again and under. I see Dad standing at the sitting-room side of the door. I see him in his armchair in the field in Connemara. I see you both at a threshold, one stumbling forward and collapsing; the other falling backward and under. Slick as sealskin, thrashing and struggling to try to swim to the surface, to escape the murky depths and surge towards the light.

You died as you had lived – in the middle of a huge adventure, diving into the great unknown – but now you are still. I've put you back together, perhaps clumsily, perhaps not paying enough attention to detail, but you are back together, body part by body part, animated, yourself, always. I have dissected, examined, sliced through your insides, so that everything that was pushed down, buried, suppressed, is now exposed; so that I can make you be still. And now that I have put you back together, told your story, described you completely, I will have to finally let you go.

Acknowledgements

Sincere thanks to Marianne Gunn O'Connor – my agent and friend of almost twenty years. To Alison Walsh for making sense of my jumbled thoughts and highly disorganised notes. To Christine Doran, expert overseer of every word that I write.

To Joe DeSouza, Caroline Osborne, Judy Kelly and Nick Kelly for early and invaluable inspiration.

Thanks also to my extraordinary godmother, Rosemary Comyn, for her early memories of Mum, her exquisite turn of phrase and her endless encouragement and support.

To the Arts Council and to Sarah Bannan Keegan in particular for her faith and support.

To the Royal Literary Society for much-welcome financial assistance.

To Kip Carroll for author photo and friendship and to Brian Blackwell for helping me to focus.

Thanks to Dominique Kennedy, Honorary Consul General of Ireland in Quito, Ecuador, for her incredible help and information. To Sari Kelly and David Kelly for early interviews.

To Trina Vargo of the US Ireland Alliance, and to Marlene Ffrench for helping me in every way.

To Conor Ferguson for cover inspiration and to Yvonne Moore for creative input.

To all the wonderful human beings at New Island, who have made this the best publishing experience I've ever had: Des Doyle, Mariel Deegan, Aoife K. Walsh, Cassia Gaden Gilmartin, Michael Darcy, Mary Deegan and Tom Jordan. Special thanks to Djinn von Noorden for her exceptional editing, her belief in me and in *Still* and for her valued friendship.

Last but most importantly, thanks to Carrie Nathan and all my treasured friends, to my siblings for not just agreeing to my writing about our adored mum but for actively supporting this work from its outset. To Garvan Grant – for making everything lighter, warmer and better.

And to my brilliant, brave, bright and beautiful Ruby Mae for amazing and inspiring me every single day.